**ATE DUE**

|  |  |  |  |  |  |
|---|---|---|---|---|---|
|  |  |  |  |  |  |
|  |  |  |  |  |  |
|  |  |  |  |  |  |
|  |  |  |  |  |  |
|  |  |  |  |  |  |
|  |  |  |  |  |  |
|  |  |  |  |  |  |
|  |  |  |  |  |  |
|  |  |  |  |  |  |
|  |  |  |  |  |  |

# The Landscape of Memory

# THE LANDSCAPE OF MEMORY

## BY MILTON MELTZER

Viking Kestrel

VIKING KESTREL
Viking Penguin Inc., 40 West 23rd Street, New York, New York 10010, U.S.A.
Penguin Books Ltd, Harmondsworth, Middlesex, England
Penguin Books Australia Ltd, Ringwood, Victoria, Australia
Penguin Books Canada Limited, 2801 John Street,
Markham, Ontario, Canada L3R 1B4
Penguin Books (N.Z.) Ltd, 182–190 Wairau Road, Auckland 10, New Zealand

First published in 1987 by Viking Penguin Inc.
Published simultaneously in Canada

LIBRARY OF CONGRESS CATALOGING IN PUBLICATION DATA
Meltzer, Milton,     The landscape of memory.
Summary: Discusses how memory works and examines what we remember and why
we forget.
1. Memory—Juvenile literature. [1. Memory] I. Title.
BF371.M44 1987     153.1'2     86-32406     ISBN 0-670-80821-0

Printed in the United States of America by
The Book Press, Brattleboro, Vt.
Set in Trump.

1   2   3   4   5   91   90   89   88   87

*For the new Benjamin*

# CONTENTS

# The Landscape of Memory

# CHAPTER I

# AN INFINITE CAPACITY

*I can hardly believe some things in my own landscape of memory.* —ALFRED KAZIN

*"'Tis a poor sort of memory that only works backwards," the Queen remarked.* —LEWIS CARROLL

*Everything fades, save memory.* —ALBERT CAMUS

You probably think you have a poor memory. You don't remember your friend's telephone number, you forget your mother's birthday, you can't recall the year the Civil War started. But you can recognize the faces of everyone in your classes when you meet them on the street. And this, even though their faces all come pretty much the same: two eyes, a nose, a mouth, two ears, a chin, a color. You can tell the plots of many movies you've seen. You know the words and music of dozens of rock songs. You can recognize so many places you've been to before—streets, parks, playgrounds, towns, buildings, rooms.

Think, too, of all the skills you've learned and can remember how to use effortlessly: cooking, driving a car, dancing, hitting a forehand, kicking a field goal, playing the piano. And what about talking? That calls on thousands of words you've learned. Each word containing several bits of information. Yet in a conversation with a friend you speak, it seems, almost without thinking. The words pour out of your mouth, and they make sense. At almost the same moment, your friend is replying to you, making sounds you must interpret. At once you think of how to answer, put it into words, and say it. Back and forth goes the ball of conversation, with an amazing speed and efficiency that you don't even pause to notice. You are remembering ideas, feelings, facts, images, and the words with which to express them. It is a stunning, if everyday, example of what memory can do.

Even the most ordinary mind has a fantastic capacity for memory. Scientists estimate that in a lifetime the brain can store a million billion items of information. (That's 1,000,000,000,000,000 items.) It amounts to a thousand new bits of information per second of a life lived from birth to seventy-five years of age. And still, if you live that long, you'll have used only a fraction of what the memory could store.

What is memory? How is it defined? The scientists who are trying to understand memory offer a number of definitions. They all seem to agree that memory is the ability of living beings to store information about past experience so that it can be drawn upon later to serve our present needs and interests. When we remember something, we have managed to do three things: to acquire the information, to store it, and to retrieve it. When we fail to remember something, it means we have failed to do one of these three things.

We don't observe and remember the way a camera records on film the objects in front of its lens. No, memory is not objective or impersonal. The memory is not a machine, a mechanical device. It is a function of a living personality with his or her own needs, fears, and interests, and these powerfully influence what that person remembers.

This means that memory is not exact. As we will see later, several people will remember the same event quite differently. Eyewitnesses testifying in a court trial will often contradict one another. Members of a family sharing a common experience are likely not to recall it in the same way.

Thinking about memory is useful because it will help us find out how people apply their own past experience to meet the present and the future. Memory affects how well we do in school, at home, on the job. We want to know if there are different kinds of memory in everyday life, or is it all the same thing? Just what do we use the past for?

You're always using memory to define yourself, even if you're not aware of it. Who you are, your name, family, and home, you know because it's stored in your memory. You know what you've done, where you've been, how you've felt, who your friends are, in the same way. Your past defines you, shapes your present, and leads you to the future. Stop and think for a moment: What would you be without memory? You may not have thought about it much, and often can't recall the details, the specifics, of the past. But what it all adds up to is present in your head. You are the result of that past experience, stored in the memory.

Of course, you can remember some things very concretely when you choose: what you had for breakfast this morning, a phone call you made last night, a letter you must write, or an errand you must do today. You do this silently, without telling anyone. Yet you have memories that come without your seeking them—whether while awake or asleep.

In all these cases the past becomes present to you, to you alone, in your head. But you remember much that you didn't experience personally. You learn about things that happened to other people: not only family and friends and neighbors and classmates, but also people you never saw or met, and people who may have lived a hundred or a thousand years before you—historical figures. You learn from their experiences, especially when you discover that their lives have some meaning for your own.

Memory, then, is part of our everyday life. We are always summoning up our own past experience to meet the present and the future. *How* we do it—that's a question that needs much looking into. One thing we know: We don't all remember with the same degree of power.

# CHAPTER II

# THE CASE OF S

_The proper memory for a politician is one that knows what to remember and what to forget._
—JOHN MORLEY

_Those who forget the past are doomed to repeat it. But those who always remember the past often don't know when it is over, when something relevantly new has appeared._ —SIDNEY HOOK

_An injury is much sooner forgotten than an insult._
—LORD CHESTERFIELD

_There is no recollection which time does not put an end to._ —CERVANTES

There are some people whose power of memory is far beyond the normal. President Franklin D. Roosevelt's campaign manager, James A. Farley, could remember the names of twenty thousand persons met while politicking about the country. Cyrus, the Persian king, could call out of memory the names of every officer in his army as he gave them orders. Themistocles, the Greek statesman, is said to have learned the names of all the citizens of Athens.

Fabulous stories about the memories of musicians are plentiful. Arturo Toscanini, the conductor, was sent a musical score by a hopeful young composer, who got no response. Seventeen years later the two men met at a dinner party. The composer said, "I don't suppose you'd remember that I once sent you a piece of mine in the hope you'd perform it." The conductor replied that he did recall it, then went over to the piano and played it through from memory, pointing out the weaknesses that made him decide not to conduct it. Or to cite the prodigious memory of other musicians: Hans von Bülow, the German conductor, while riding the train from Hamburg to Berlin, read the score of a new symphony he had never seen or heard before, and then conducted it that evening without the score. Mozart could compose a whole symphony in his head and later write down the complete orchestration from memory. At eight, Felix Mendelssohn knew Beethoven's symphonies by heart.

For more examples we can go to preliterate societies. Here, too, can be found astonishing feats of memory. The poems of the *Iliad* and the *Odyssey*, before Homer wrote them down, were kept alive by word of mouth, stored in the memory of the ancient Greeks. Together the two Homeric poems total some twenty-seven thousand lines. In the mountains of Yugoslavia, about fifty years ago, visiting scholars recorded epic songs from the memory of the local people. Such a song was often several thousand lines long and would take hours to sing. Experienced singers knew at least thirty such songs; some claimed to know a hundred. These were not fixed and previously composed texts but followed basic themes and formulas, with the singer improvising the song anew each time he sang the oral poetry.

In the African country of Liberia, oral historians remember the history of whole clans and tribes. Some suggest that perhaps preliterate people have particularly good memories to make up for being unable to write things down. But the lack of something doesn't cause something else. Lack of wings doesn't make you faster on your feet. Rather, a particular culture nourishes particular abilities. Oral poets in a nonliterate society are raised on a specific concept of poetry. That concept of poetry changes when literacy develops, and so does the concept of memory.

The brilliant British mathematician Alexander Craig Aitken (1895–1967) had a legendary memory in many fields. He could muster a host of facts about numbers, mathematics, and mathematicians. A fine violinist, he could play many pieces by heart and identify a great deal of music when allowed to hear only snatches of it. He was able to quote at length from English literature and recite long passages of both Latin and English poetry. His recall of events he witnessed was so sharp and reliable that others drew upon his memory as though he were a record book. He was always precise about names, dates, places. In teaching, he could read just once the names of a new class of thirty-five students and never have to consult the list again. Give him a numbered line from a volume of Virgil's poetry and he could recite the words in that line— and, the converse, tell you the number of the line if you fed him the words in it.

Great chess players are often gifted with a powerful memory. Paul Charles Morphy, born in New Orleans in 1837, was a child prodigy at chess. He became world champion. He could play blindfold chess, which requires perfect recall of every new position throughout the game. He often played blindfold against several opponents at the same time, none of them blindfold. He could recall every move in every game of hundreds played in his career. About four hundred of his games are preserved in the records because, after the game ended, he was able to dictate from memory all the moves.

Chess masters have learned and store in their memory about fifty thousand patterns of positions on the board, according to the scientist Herbert A. Simon. But he adds that experts in any field probably have memorized some fifty thousand clusters of information in their specialty.

Ancient history records many feats of memory. Seneca the Elder, a Roman teacher, could repeat two thousand names in the order given him. A man named Simplicias could recite Virgil backwards. The ancients valued such mental gymnastics highly. The Greek dramatist Aeschylus called memory "the mother of all wisdom." And Cicero, the Roman statesman and orator, said, "Memory is the treasury and guardian of all things."

In the Washington, D.C., of today there is a restaurant that serves hundreds of people at lunch and at dinner. Each customer orders French gourmet food that must be prepared perfectly. The maître d'hôtel can remember specific dinners ordered over the past forty years by his customers. On any morning he can recall the orders of every customer of the day before, as well as their specific table and place setting. The capital knows Jacques Scardella for his staggering ability to match face, place, and palate.

*The New Yorker* magazine's film critic, Pauline Kael, is noted for her recall of almost every detail in movies going back to her early childhood. When she sees revivals of old pictures, she always knows what's coming in the next scene.

There are scholarly Jews who have memorized the Talmud, a compilation of Jewish law and tradition, both in its worded message and in its exact appearance on the printed page. That extraordinary feat of memory has been described by the Reverend Dr. David Philipson. There are twenty large volumes to the Babylonian Talmud, containing thousands of pages. Every printed edition has exactly the same number of pages and the same words on each page. Dr. Philipson met a Hebrew scholar from Poland who knew the whole Talmud by heart. If you opened one volume of the Talmud, say, at page 10, and placed a pin on a word, say, the fourth word in line 8, and then asked the scholar what word was in this same spot on page 38 or page 50 or any other page, pressing the pin through till it reached the desired page, he would then say the word, and it was always correct.

It meant he had visualized in his memory the entire Talmud; it was as though the pages of the Talmud were photographed upon his brain. There is some evidence that at one period the Talmud was handed down solely by memory. Perhaps the feat of such Jews is the survival of a custom among early Jewish students in many communities of Eastern Europe.

How unique is such a memory? It is by no means as rare as one would guess, says the neurologist Ulric Neisser. He refers to frequent secondhand reports of people with astonishing memory for pictures, musical scores, chess positions, business transactions, dramatic scripts, or faces. Most often, he adds, you hear of a kind of visual memory that enables one to recall whole pages of a book that's been read. Many people report having had that ability in early life, but of losing it by the end of their teens.

Psychologists have come across quite a few people they call "calendar calculators." They can tell what day of the week corresponds to a given date in the past. One example was a minister named Dryden W. Phelps, who lived in the late nineteenth and early twentieth centuries. He could recall some particular thing that had happened on any day of the last sixty years of his life, and do it immediately upon request. For instance, if he were asked what happened on March 6, 1879, in a few moments he would state what day of the week that was—Monday or Thursday or whatever—then give the weather for that day and describe some particular thing that happened.

People with "photographic memory" are often heard of. There are quite a few examples of the remarkable ability to store visual information in the memory. A woman who taught at Harvard and was a skilled artist had that ability. She could project an exact image of a picture or a scene on her mental screen. The image kept all the detailed surface and color of the original. The image would remain still, as though fixed on canvas, permitting her to examine its every aspect.

The power of her visual recall was not confined to pictures. Long after reading a poem in a foreign language, she could recall how the poem looked on the printed page and write it out rapidly from the bottom line to the top line, reading it off the screen of her mind's eye.

This visual recall is known as eidetic imagery. The word "eidetic" comes from the Greek *eidos*, meaning "form" or "that which is seen." It seems to be found more often in children than in adults. Perhaps 5 to 10 percent of children have it. Such children can remember whole scenes with great accuracy, though the capacity generally fades in the adult years—why, no one knows.

Actually, eidetic imagery can be more than photographic. Some people have that kind of recall by ear. They can hear a whole symphony in their mind, with the full range of instruments playing. And some may have a tactile eidetic image. With their touch recall they can feel the texture of a sable fur in all its richness.

But "there is such a thing as too good a memory," warns Frederick K. Goodwin, research chief of the National Institute of Mental Health. Certain fears, phobias, obsessions, can overpower the personality with memories that are terribly damaging. Perhaps the most famous case of harm done by a memory that never fails is the story of "S."

S was a Russian, Solomon V. Shereshevskii, a young newspaper reporter in Moscow. In the early 1920s his editor sent him for a psychological evaluation. Nothing seemed wrong with his personality and he did his job well. But his memory amazed his co-workers. When he covered a story, his mind retained everything he observed—from the important to the most trivial details, including names, phone numbers, addresses— and all this without taking notes.

At the clinic the reporter was examined by Aleksandr Luria, an eminent psychologist, intensely interested in memory. Given all kinds of memory tests, S never failed them. Luria studied S from the 1920s to the 1950s, writing a classic book about the case called *The Mind of a Mnemonist.* (A mnemonist is one who has acquired skills helping one to remember something. The word comes from the Greek *mneme*, the goddess of memory.)

Luria found no limit to the capacity of S's memory or to the length of time he retained a memory. S could recall testing sessions he had taken thirty years before, repeating a series of random numbers or letters memorized on that much earlier date. S changed jobs from time to time, shifting from reporter to efficiency expert to financial analyst and finally to professional mnemonist, making a living by public exhibitions of his amazing ability.

Luria soon learned that S remembered far better than most, and he had a special way of doing it. How? British psychologist Ian L. M. Hunter describes the method:

He used the classical mnemonist's technique of imagining richly vivid, concrete mental pictures, which he arranged in a chain of pairs. If given a 25-word list he might take an imaginary walk along a street that has a vivid succession of landmarks. He would represent the first word by a distinctively imaged picture which he would "locate" on the first landmark, and so on. During a single, and not too rapid, presentation of the word list, he would progressively devise such a chain of images that was extremely rich in perception-like properties. This would result in accurate, durable memorization. Even years afterwards, he would be able to recapitulate the chain of images, and so recall the list of words in either forward or backward sequence.

Such a superhuman memory became not a blessing but a curse. S was deeply upset because he could not forget what he had memorized in his performances. To escape the burden, he tried writing down the material and then burning the paper, but that did not drop it out of his mind. When he was talking to a friend, any word exchanged might evoke a flood of irrelevant or trivial memories that poured off his tongue and made him sound almost crazy. These undesired memories tripped him up, so that he could never stick to a single line of conversation. He dragged after him an unbelievable load of useless information. The biggest problem of his life was that he could not forget.

The story of S makes us recall what psychologist William James once said: "If we remembered every-thing we should be as ill as if we remembered nothing."

# CHAPTER III

# WHAT WE REMEMBER, WHY WE FORGET

*Memories lurk like dustballs at the backs of drawers.*

—JAY MCINERNEY

*How strange are the tricks of memory, which, often hazy as a dream about the most important events of a man's life, religiously preserve the merest trifles.*

—RICHARD BURTON

*My memory is very good. I can make the same mistakes today that I made fifty years ago.*

—SIMON ROTHSCHILD

*Vanity plays lurid tricks with our memory.*

—JOSEPH CONRAD

Memory is often thought of as simply the ability to recall the past. But the past—meaning time gone by—has many different kinds of things lodged in it. For one, things that happened to you: breaking a leg in a football game, starting school, moving to a new house, any event in your life. Another kind of memory is for facts: July 4, 1776, the date of the Declaration of Independence, the fact that Alexander Graham Bell invented the telephone. These aren't things that happened to you, but facts you picked up in school or by reading or watching TV, or wherever.

Then there is memory for the meaning of something. You remember that "bee" means a winged insect that depends upon pollen or nectar for food, or that "nasty" means something dirty or foul that disgusts you. There are many thousands of such words whose meanings you remember. Another kind of memory is for what your senses tell you. Faces—you recall a great many you've seen, whether intimately or just passing on the street. And the smell of your mother's kreplach or cabbage soup, the sound of the music playing when you knew you were falling in love, the taste of a persimmon.

A different kind of memory is the one we seem to be born with. The infant "remembers" to suck at its mother's breast; everyone "remembers" how to sleep, breathe, and digest. Such memories are inherited. They are stored in our genes.

Some scientists now think these various kinds of memory fall into two distinct memory systems. One system controls fact knowledge: the ability to provide names, dates, faces, baseball scores. The other system involves skill knowledge: how to ride a bicycle, drive a car, or hit a backhand.

The two forms of memory are thought to reside in different parts of the brain, say the researchers, and may be under different biochemical control. They may also have arisen separately in the long course of evolution. These ideas come from observation of victims of amnesia, the inability to remember any new fact knowledge since their memory loss began, as a result of a stroke or an injury to the head. The skill memories are rarely lost or forgotten in such patients. How strong the distinction is between the two memory systems is not certain. There are clear differences, the scientists say, but they don't know how much the systems share and how they are separate.

The fact knowledge that amnesia victims lose is often called "short-term memory." An example of it is looking up a number in the phone book, remembering it long enough to dial it, and then promptly forgetting it. One explanation is that we are aware of the information the brain processes just deeply enough to use it at the moment. Then we stop thinking about it and it drops from the memory system. That we know we will forget some kinds of information quickly leads us to rehearse it if we think we'll want to retain it longer. We say to ourselves over and over again the phone number or the address or the name we want to remember. That may move it from short-term into long-term memory.

The theory behind this holds that memory has several parts or stages. Input from the senses to the brain enters an immediate memory, which holds it for about half a second. Certain selected items from the immediate memory may then pass to the short-term memory, where they hang on for several seconds to a few hours. That's because we can keep active only so much material at one time. New items coming into the short-term memory will drive out items already there. That's why the rehearsal of what we want to hold shuts out new data and prolongs memory of the old.

Items that move into the long-term memory persist perhaps a few days and then may become permanent memory, spanning a life's experience. They include memory of past events as well as of the meaning of events and objects. Long-term memory is the major part of human memory, the storehouse for our knowledge of the world and our experiences in it. Such knowledge has several elements. It includes ideas about the nature of things—abstract like "liberty" or concrete like "bed"—and the words or labels for those ideas.

Another type of knowledge we store, mentioned earlier, is used to perform motor acts. Alicia de Larrocha, for example, retains the sequence of finger and hand movements needed to perform a Mozart piano concerto. John McEnroe retains the sequence of movements he needs to serve the tennis ball over the net. Neurologists have performed many kinds of experiments to try to determine how the brain processes or organizes knowledge in short- and long-term memory.

There seems to be something quite different about new memories and old ones. Some scientists explain this by the idea of memory consolidation. They say newly formed memories are delicate and easily disturbed, while older memories have become sturdy enough to resist anything short of brain damage. New memories need time to wear themselves into the brain, to make permanent tracks, so to speak, perhaps through biochemical changes in brain tissue.

Some researchers, on the other hand, believe it is better to avoid any distinction between the short- and long-term, because the one mechanism seems to merge so imperceptibly into the other. Whether something is remembered for a long or short time or not at all depends upon many different circumstances that can't be told apart.

Not remembering at all brings us to the problem of forgetting. If the brain is almost unlimited in its capacity, why then do we appear to forget? Think of memory as a recording system coupled to a playback system. How does the mind then summon up data encoded and stored in its memory circuits?

It usually starts with a cue, a question someone asks you or you ask yourself. Let's say the teacher asks you to name the sixteenth President of the United States. The retrieval process, one researcher writes, might go something like this:

> You may be able to retrieve this directly, or you may generate some cues of your own—16th President sounds familiar, must be famous, might have occurred 90 years or more after the Union was formed, given the usual Presidential term of 4 to 8 years. You might do an orderly search through the set of Presidents or a less directed search, just generating Presidents in the hope that you will realize one was the 16th.
>
> For each candidate President, you have to make a decision as to whether it is the desired response. Washington certainly isn't; Grant might be. Finally you decide, "16th President, that's the Civil War guy, what was his name?"—ultimately generating the called-for response, "Abraham Lincoln."

In this challenge to memory, it's clear the person knew something but wasn't sure of it. There are lots of things we know and can recall right off. There are many we think we know but can't recall this minute, others about which we're not sure, many that we don't know and know we don't know. And there are many that we think we don't know—but realize later that we do. This has to do with our awareness of what's stored in the memory.

To retrieve something from that memory is a complex process. The cue to make a search of memory can come from inside, like a pleasant smell that stirs hunger and leads us to remember when we last ate a meal. Some information that turns up in the search of memory may be data we weren't looking for. Asked to remember a certain person in an old neighborhood, you may clearly remember the face but can't recall the name, although you suddenly remember the name of the policeman on the block. So you've gone some distance in retrieval, but not all the way.

One theory of why we forget suggests that the particular memory we are looking for can't be distinguished from all the other memory traces in the brain. The trace itself hasn't necessarily faded. But as more and more bits of information are gathered and stored, particularly those with similar associations or similar meaning, it becomes harder to recall the original material. The memories are said to interfere with one another. This isn't because the storehouse is overcrowded with memories, but rather because new experiences, changed habits of thought, and the like, break the connections or cues that helped us to tell one memory from another and retrieve the trace.

Others ask if failure to remember over the years means that there has actually been a loss of the memory trace itself, as in the melting of an ice cube. The memory simply decays and disappears.

Making a search in your head for a memory often means putting more and more cues together. If they finally add up, then you haven't forgotten. Forgetting happens as more and more memories pile up without enough cues to single out what you're after. If you've been thinking for some time about a certain area of knowledge, then you're less likely to forget a memory linked to it. Your mind has been warmed up for the particular task to come.

We all know those times when we're asked about something in our long-term memory—a word, a name, an experience—and we can't fish up the answer right away, but say, "It's on the tip of my tongue!" Often the first letter or even the first syllable of the word desired may be known, but we still can't recall it. In our mind, we run through all the words in that category beginning with the initial letter in the hope of remembering the right word. And we're still not able to call it up. No matter how hard we try, the memory stubbornly resists our effort. "Just give me a little time," we say; "it'll come back." What sometimes happens is that our mind thinks sideways about it, recalling some slightly related item, and then the right word swims happily into view. The explanation may be that we've reached the memory trace by a different neural pathway.

We find we can remember some things easily; others

are harder. You don't try to remember what was in the comic strip you saw in this morning's paper, but if asked, you could recall it easily, at least for a while. And you could repeat what a girlfriend or boyfriend told you in confidence last week. What about the new French vocabulary you studied in class the other day? Or a new phone number you called? Or the name of a stranger you were just introduced to? That's often not so easy. Some students can reel off the career statistics of a ballplayer's performance with no trouble, yet fail to remember yesterday's math lesson. What makes some things easy to remember and some more difficult?

This brings us to a basic question: How do people remember things? For the answer to this, and many other questions raised, we need to know something about the human brain, that mass of nerve tissue no bigger than our fist.

# CHAPTER IV

# THE THREE-POUND MARVEL

*Memory is the thing you forget with.*
—ALEXANDER CHASE

*Memory is a net; one finds it full of fish when he takes it from the brook; but a dozen miles of water have run through it without sticking.*
—OLIVER WENDELL HOLMES, SR.

*Everyone complains of his memory, and no one complains of his judgment.*
—LA ROCHEFOUCAULD

A dull-looking thing, the brain, but it is the most important organ we have. It weighs only about three pounds. Packed into its small gray mass within the skull are ten to fifteen thousand million nerve cells. The connections between the nerve cells—called "synapses"—number some one hundred million million. About the same number of glial cells support and nourish the nerve cells.

There is nothing exciting about how the human brain looks. Viewing it, you can't tell what abilities it has, what thought or memory it is capable of. Yet it is the brain, not the heart or any other organ, that has made us. In it lies the power to compose music, design a nuclear missile, or make peace. It is probably the most complex system known in the universe.

Only recently in human history did we begin to study the brain, to try to find out what it is and how it works. As late as 1800, long after the birth of modern science, very little accurate information about the brain had been recorded. Yet it was the brain that gave us the intelligence for a vast number of remarkable achievements long before then.

There are many firsts claimed in brain research. Around 500 B.C., a Greek named Alcmaeon was the first to say the brain was the organ of intelligence. Soon after came several men who tried to describe the parts of the brain. They were not sure which parts did what. Then for a thousand years, held back by religious beliefs and ancient traditions, people did little research. Not until the Renaissance and the inquiring minds of men such as Leonardo da Vinci (1452–1519) and Andreas Vesalius (1514–1564) did men look at the human anatomy and describe it. They drew pictures of the brain, stressing this part or that, and often doing it quite wrongly. People sometimes are more influenced by what they think they should see than by what is actually before their eyes.

In the 1800s, the pace of research picked up remarkably. Anatomy and physiology advanced on a wide front, aided by the microscope and the camera. Experiments on the surface layers of the brain, the cortex, revealed that that was where cerebral function is centered. It took nearly 2,500 years—from the time of Alcmaeon—for the modern era of brain research to arrive. Now the anatomy of the brain is no longer guesswork or dogma but facts discovered, tested, and written down.

Important as it is, we are not going to spend time describing the parts of the brain. They are very numerous and complex and have been given Greek, Latin, and English names, with many parts called by the names of their explorers.

It took millions of years of evolution for the brain to develop. Evolution from fish to amphibian to reptile to mammal to primate seems (but isn't) logical and purposeful. The brain arrived almost by accident. Other species developed different organs to great size. The enlargement of the human brain was small by comparison, but the added pound or two of nerve tissue made a tremendous difference. Of all the animal species, the one with the largest brain mass for its body weight is *Homo sapiens*—ourselves. It gave our species great potential power.

It was about 100,000 years ago that the brain reached its present size, judging by fossils. That makes our brain a prehistoric brain. The simple hunter-gatherer, the early caveman, the Stone Age farmer, all had the same brain we have. So it is not further changes in the brain but cultural inheritance that makes us what we are today. The brain began to reap its potential when population increased, larger and more settled communities grew up, and division of labor developed. Although the brain of one person is much like that of another, abilities vary considerably. Some people live a routine existence that shows little use of intelligence. Others can write a great novel, compose a superb symphony, design a computer or city, calculate the movements of a solar system.

This difference in abilities is linked to the enormous range of the brain's possibilities. Nerve cells are the brain's basic units, but the variety of interconnections between them is probably infinite. That is why no two people—even identical twins raised together—can ever be exactly alike. What we are capable of has nothing to do with size; people with bigger brains are not the wiser for it. The size of the brain most of us have is more than suited to our needs. The problem is how to realize its potential.

There is no organ in the human body as complex as the brain. It takes longer than any other organ to reach full growth. The adult brain consists of some 13 billion cells. Ten billion of those cells are developed within the first five months in the mother's womb. Those billions of cells must last for the rest of life. If injured, they do not grow back or mend, nor do they reproduce. In the last few months of pregnancy, the brain develops rapidly in the womb. After birth, the brain's growth slows down, coming to a stop at about age five.

This is why poor nutrition for a pregnant mother can be a disaster for the baby she carries. If the unborn child gets too little protein and other nutrients, the brain, in many cases, is stunted; the baby is permanently handicapped. And if the baby is not fed properly during the first five years of life, when the brain can still grow, the child will come to maturity with its brain power significantly below normal.

Modern research into the brain finds that it does more than control behavior. It is the monitor and governor of every aspect of body function and chemistry.

But how does the human brain work? That is the central problem the scientists seek to answer. It is, in fact, one of the deepest questions of all modern science. It is the brain struggling to understand itself.

In recent years, the ways of understanding the brain have changed dramatically. The idea that you could localize functions of the brain dominated science a hundred years ago. It guided brain research for the next fifty years. Then research shifted from anatomy to neurochemistry—the chemistry of the nervous system. Important links were established between neurochemistry and psychology. Many psychological observations could be explained at least in part by the way the physiology of the nervous system operated. There is still a long way to go for researchers to find out:

>How connections are established within the brain.

>What kinds of information are handled at those connections.

>How that information is processed.

Which means the greatest challenge remains: How does the brain store memories?

# CHAPTER V

# COULD WE LIVE WITHOUT IT?

*Remember this day, in which ye came out from Egypt, out of the house of bondage.*          —EXODUS

*What memory has in common with art is the knack for selection, the taste for detail. . . . Memory contains precise details, not the whole picture; highlights, if you will, not the entire show. . . . More than anything, memory resembles a library in alphabetical disorder, and with no collected works by anyone.*

—JOSEPH BRODSKY

*Everybody needs his memories. They keep the wolf of insignificance from the door.*          —SAUL BELLOW

If we don't yet know how the brain stores memories, we do know that the ability of the human mind to learn is the result of that mysterious capacity. Without it, language, thought, knowledge, culture—all that makes us human—would be impossible.

Yet non–human beings also have the ability to store and recall information. Almost all creatures have been proved capable of memory. Even single-celled animals learn from experience. They demonstrate their most simple and basic kind of memory by an improved reaction to repeated stimuli. Without some form of memory, they couldn't benefit from experience. It means that repeated events have an effect upon the nervous system that records them and reacts to them.

The simpler animals with far fewer nerve cells are studied by scientists because it's much harder to tackle the human with his or her billions of brain cells.

A German biologist some eighty years ago worked with an intestinal parasitic worm that has exactly 162 nerve cells. His experiments showed that the worm could learn, had a memory, and acted on the information it stored. The honey bee, with 7,000 neurons, is capable of many more functions, including some beyond us humans—flying, for instance.

But the human memory makes an enormous leap beyond this. Its ability to store and retrieve information is of quite a different order from that of such simple animals. Yet we don't know how much of the three pounds of nerve tissue in our skulls is used in memory. Nor do we even know much about which parts are the main ones involved. We assume that the information is somehow stored by the process of learning, and, as we suggested before, is remembered by retrieval. What we call the memory is the information in storage.

Thousands of years ago, people tried to figure out what memory is. Plato, the Greek philosopher of the fourth century B.C., suggested the wax tablet idea. He thought impressions are recorded on the mind the way lines are etched on wax surfaces by a pointed instrument. As time passes, he said, the impression wears off: We forget.

Many other ideas about the physical basis of memory have been offered since that remote time. In the early 1900s, one theory held that a memory trace was a particular pathway among neurons. New memories laid down their traces as new connections were made between neurons. But that theory was rejected when other evidence disproved it. A more recent theory holds that specific memories may reside, not in a particular synapse or pathway or molecule, but in the pattern of electrical and chemical changes over the brain as a whole. The pursuit of various lines of research goes on daily in laboratories around the world.

A neurobiologist at Harvard Medical School, Dr. David H. Hubel, suggests a very simple way to look at how the brain works. He says:

> In brief, there is an input: man's only way of knowing about the outside world. There is an output: man's only way of responding to the outside world and influencing it. And between input and output there is everything else, which must include perception, emotions, memory, thought and whatever else makes man human.

In spite of recent advances in technique, most parts of the brain are still dimly understood. New and revolutionary methods are badly needed. The difficulty of research into the living brain is obvious. You couldn't study the signals of single cells in it without opening the skull on the operating table. And, of course, that can't be done for ethical reasons. Nevertheless, researchers do make advances in getting at some of the higher functions of the brain.

Using lower animals with far simpler nervous systems than a human's, researchers have poked into individual cells, using microelectrodes. They have shown that, as Dr. Hubel says, "when an animal learns or forgets a response, changes take place in the transmission of signals across particular synapses. The learning here is obviously of a simple kind, but it appears to be true learning." Such discoveries have in the past often been extended to higher forms of life.

Serious attention is being paid to memory because it has a fundamental role. The ability to remember is not some minor aspect of our nature. If we lost taste or speech, it would be a handicap, but we could still live like most other people. We'd eat somewhat differently and tell what's on our mind not by speech but through signs or written words. But deprived of memory? We'd be very strange. Memory is so basic a part of intelligence, of learning, of consciousness, that it is almost impossible to think of living without it. A better understanding of it will come along when neurology uncovers the secrets of the nervous system.

Since scientists as yet can't say what memory really is, they try to suggest what it is like. They have compared memory to a kind of muscle that can be strengthened through exercise, or to a kind of writing or recording. (Remember Plato's notion of the wax tablet?) A third comparison pictures memory as a reference book or library. And a fourth views memory as though it were a computer where bits of information are stored by some coding system.

None of these metaphors has proved satisfactory. We do store a great variety of material, including sounds, words, images, and ideas. But how we store them and where, and how we retrieve them—these questions are still unanswered. It is generally agreed that the two hemispheres of the brain are somewhat specialized, with, to put it broadly, reason on the left half and feeling on the right. But that distinction isn't at all firm, for information of all sorts moves back and forth from one half of the brain to the other. Each half can store things the other half seems to specialize in. Nor are most kinds of memory stored in any single part of the brain. Research suggests, rather, that memories are spread widely in the brain through interconnected sets of patterns.

So however we do remember, it isn't like any metaphor imagined up to now, but by some far more complex system that our minds have yet to figure out. We nonscientists take memory so casually because from our earliest days we have used it so effortlessly. The possibility of losing it seems like some freaky twist in a science fiction plot. But damage to the brain can make it a frightening reality at any moment.

# CHAPTER VI

# THE CRUELEST DISEASE

*Memories are like stones. Time and distance erode them like acid.* —UGO BETTI

*In remembrance resides the secret of redemption.* —THE BAAL SHEM-TOV

*It is a curious fact that in bad days we can very vividly recall the good time that is now no more; but that in good days we have only a very cold and imperfect memory of the bad.* —SCHOPENHAUER

*You have to begin to lose your memory, if only in bits and pieces, to realize that memory is what makes our lives. Life without memory is no life at all. . . . Our memory is our coherence, our reason, our feeling, even our action. Without it, we are nothing. . . .*

This passage is from the memoirs of the Spanish film director Luis Buñuel. It makes us ask what sort of world a man lives in who has lost the greater part of his memory. Some idea can be gained from the classic example of H.M., who became the victim of epilepsy, a seizure disorder, at the age of sixteen. When drugs didn't help, his doctors became desperate. They had to try something, anything, that would stop his almost daily seizures, which threatened his life.

When H.M. was twenty-seven, surgery was done on his brain to remove the front parts of both temporal lobes. The surgery ended the seizures, but something else was now terribly wrong. H.M. couldn't find his room. He couldn't recognize the doctors and nurses taking care of him. When someone was introduced to him, he forgot the person's name and face within minutes. He could not remember his own new experiences. Yet his earlier memories, his life experiences before surgery, were intact and normal.

That was more than thirty years ago. H.M. has been studied carefully ever since his surgery. In the 1980s, he still did not know where he lived, who took care of him, what he ate at his last meal. He couldn't find his way in his own neighborhood, or remember faces or phone numbers or even his own age. He would read the same newspaper over and over again, a striking sign of the failure of his brain to record or preserve new memory traces. When given a seven-digit number to remember and recite, he could do it perfectly if he repeated the number as soon as he heard it. But with a slight delay between hearing and repeating, he would fail. He had lost the ability to learn new things.

But he still has a normal memory for motor skills, perhaps because those skills involve different mechanisms of memory than those of language. Scientists studying him put it this way:

> Imagine being H.M.'s tennis instructor. You would have to reintroduce yourself each lesson.

Suppose H.M. had learned a slice serve from you and did not know how to do it or what it was called before his operation. Each lesson you would have to tell him all over again what a slice serve is. But you would not have to teach him the motions, how to do it. He will learn the actual skill—his slice serve will improve with practice and remain with him as well as it does for other pupils. He just can't remember what it is called or anything you said about it, or, for that matter, who you are. From his point of view, you are a stranger in a new setting each time he takes his tennis lesson.

The surgery on H.M. removed a part of his brain called the hippocampus. There are two of these structures, one on each side of the brain, on each temporal lobe. When just one is taken out, it doesn't seem to interfere much with memory. But in H.M.'s case, both were removed. As a result of H.M.'s tragic loss, this type of brain surgery has not been done again.

H.M. knows he lives always in the present. He wonders whether he has just done or said something wrong. At the moment, things may look clear to him. But what happened a few minutes ago? It worries him all the time.

A golfer we shall call Harold offers another example of memory loss. He plays the game well, but he forgets where the ball lands and forgets the score after each hole. "Oh, amnesia," we say, "that's his trouble." That word comes from the Greek for forgetfulness. But there are many forms of memory loss and many causes of it. A punch to the head, a bullet wound, falling off a bike, or a car accident can bring it about. Knocked unconscious, the victim may suffer a temporary or permanent loss of memory—or no amnesia at all. Sometimes earlier memory, seconds or an hour before the injury, is erased, and other times memory covering seconds or an hour after the event is prevented for a time. The two don't necessarily go together.

In some people, memory loss following physical injury is not limited to personal identity. One patient forgot not only his own past history but general information, such as the capital of France and the author of *Hamlet.* Another amnesic patient had to be taught all over again such basic skills as reading, writing, and counting.

Not only injury, but illness, can cause memory loss. An infection can lead to it, lack of proper nutrition, small strokes, tumors, depression, hysteria, alcoholism. And some say, while others disagree, the very process of aging.

One illness that affects memory is called Korsakoff's syndrome. S. S. Korsakoff was a Russian psychiatrist who first described the disorder in 1887. A century of further research has enriched medical knowledge of the condition. In people who have drunk to excess over many years, alcohol destroys neurons in a tiny but crucial part of the brain, leaving the rest of it perfectly preserved. Only memory is affected. The patient cannot hold on to what has been learned. New informa-

tion passes out of his or her mind like water slipping
through a sieve. Everything is forgotten as soon as it is
said or seen, though long-established memories may
remain intact.

The case of a memoryless man called Jimmie R. was
recently described by the neurologist Oliver Sacks. A
cheerful, friendly man, looking handsome and healthy,
Jimmie was first observed in 1975, when he was forty-
nine. His Korsakoff's amnesia had erased memory and
time back to 1945. He could remember his childhood
and youth vividly and in detail, up through his experiences in the Navy in World War II. When he was recalling that early life, his speech was lively and in the
present tense, as though he were living it now. But
asked during an interview what his age was, the gray-
haired man said it was nineteen. Asked what year this
was, he answered 1945.

His intelligence tested very well. He was quick and
logical and could solve complex problems and puz-
zles—if they could be done quickly. When some time
was needed, he forgot what he was doing. In just a few
seconds, he forgot whatever was said or shown or done
to him. Dr. Sacks wrote in his notes that Jimmie "is
isolated in a single moment of being, with a moat . . . of
forgetting all round him. . . . He is a man without a past
(or future), stuck in a constantly changing, meaningless moment . . . a man without roots, or rooted
only in the remote past. . . . How could he connect?
What was life without connection?"

Alcoholics who develop Korsakoff's severe memory

disorder are likely to suffer it for the remainder of their lives. Long-term, heavy drinking is the most familiar cause of brain damage that results in some kind of memory loss. But it is not the only cause. Recently another illness that cripples memory has gained wide public attention. Here is how Luis Buñuel saw its effect upon his mother:

> During the last ten years of her life, my mother gradually lost her memory. When I went to see her in Saragossa, where she lived with my brothers, I watched the way she read magazines, turning the pages carefully, one by one, from the first to the last. When she finished, I'd take the magazine from her, then give it back, only to see her leaf through it again, slowly, page by page.
>
> In the end she no longer recognized her children. She didn't know who we were, or who she was. I'd walk into her room, kiss her, sit with her awhile. Sometimes I'd leave, then turn around and walk back in again. She greeted me with the same smile and invited me to sit down—as if she were seeing me for the first time. She didn't remember my name.

Those symptoms are typical of Alzheimer's disease, a brain disorder. It usually occurs after age sixty-five, though it can strike in the forties. It afflicts up to 3 million Americans; about 7 percent of the 27 million people over sixty-five are severely disabled by the disease. Many well-known Americans have suffered it:

E. B. White, whose classic children's books *Stuart Little, Charlotte's Web* and *The Trumpet of the Swan* are widely read; the actress Rita Hayworth; the mystery writer Ross MacDonald; the artist Norman Rockwell.

The causes of Alzheimer's are not yet known, though scientists are moving ahead in analyzing the biochemical processes of the brain that may account for it. Meanwhile, the disease remains irreversible. It afflicts every ethnic and socioeconomic group and takes more than 120,000 lives a year. It is now the fourth-leading cause of death among the old, after heart disease, cancer, and stroke. On the average, victims survive six to eight years, though some linger as long as twenty.

It is the cruelest disease, for in a sense, it kills its victims twice. The mind dies first—names, places, dates wash away. The simplest tasks—telling time, finding the way about the kitchen, tying a shoelace, buttering a slice of bread—become impossible. And then the body dies. The victim loses the ability to walk, to control bodily functions, and gradually sinks into coma and death.

The disease is disastrous to the families of victims. As they struggle to provide continuous care, they are driven to physical and emotional exhaustion. They know the anguish of seeing a loved one turned into a witless stranger who no longer remembers who they are. And the crushing task of caring for a doomed patient—if they are neither rich nor poor—may eat up all their savings and more.

It was only recently that medicine began to pay serious attention to Alzheimer's. The neurology textbooks just twenty-five years ago gave only a page to it. But as the disease relentlessly extended its reach, it roused public concern. Research centers and the grants to support their work have expanded. And better investigative methods are supplying clues to what causes memory and judgment to disintegrate.

Loss of memory in the elderly was once called "senile dementia" and blamed on poor blood circulation to the brain. It was said to come inevitably with getting old. But in 1907, Alois Alzheimer, a German neurologist, reported on a woman patient with the typical symptoms who was only fifty-one. After her death, he examined her brain and found in it flat patches, or plaques, probably the location of dead nerve cells, and clumps of twisted nerve-cell fibers he called "neurofibrillary tangles." These seem to clog the neural network, fouling up the normal functions of the brain. His discovery was not given much attention for many years because his case was dismissed as "presenile" and rare. Not until the 1960s did scientists find the same tangles in the brain tissue of elderly patients with the typical symptoms.

Decay of neurons occurs normally in the human brain. But in Alzheimer's or similar diseases, there is a more rapid rate of neuronal dropout. And it affects mostly those areas of the brain important for memory and other intellectual functions.

Now it's thought that Alzheimer's is behind about

half the cases with these symptoms. The other half are usually caused by a series of small strokes that damage brain tissue, or by other conditions that cause mental confusion, such as anemia, depression, alcoholism, thyroid disease, or certain vitamin deficiencies. It means diagnosis must be careful to distinguish between these conditions, for some are treatable, and some are not.

Although no cure for Alzheimer's has been discovered as yet, its victims can be helped to a degree. Their families got together with scientists to form the Alzheimer's Disease and Related Disorders Association (ADRDA). It has organized more than 125 chapters across the country and sponsors hundreds of local self-help groups. Its newletter, research reports, books, pamphlets, and films provide much-needed guidance and encouragement.

We come back to the question of aging. Does aging in itself have an effect upon memory? Not much is understood about the process of aging in general. The life span of people in developed countries grows longer and longer. Now it is over seventy years. But the greatest age people live to remains about one hundred years. That life span for humans suggests there may be a built-in factor limiting our age.

For a long time it was said that a weakening of mental powers, including memory, went along with normal aging. But that fear now seems much exaggerated. People tend to confuse normal aging with the severe symptoms of diseases such as Alzheimer's. It's become clear that older people with such diseases are not aging normally, but are diseased. Remember, only 7 percent of those over sixty-five have Alzheimer's. And the symptoms are identical in younger people.

There are so many popular errors about the decay of mind and memory. The elderly think they alone forget names and faces. But people do that at any age and every age. When we get old, it is easy to blame the nuisance of forgetting on aging. Nor is there any proof that long-continued use of the brain wears out the neurons. Mental alertness persists into extreme old age for many people. The great artists are only the most obvious examples: Pablo Picasso, Pablo Casals, Artur Rubinstein, Titian, Chagall, Toscanini, Verdi, Frank Lloyd Wright. . . . And tests show old people can learn new tasks as well as the young.

Experiments also cast strong doubt on another memory myth: that the elderly have trouble remembering events in the recent past, but recall the remote past vividly. Many experiments show the loss to be fairly uniform across the years since the experience. Both the elderly and young adults recalled the more remote events more poorly than recent events.

The word "senility" comes from the Latin for "old age." It shouldn't have been twisted into meaning doddering old fools or crazy people. Old people are just old, unless proved otherwise.

# CHAPTER VII

# THE MEMORY PALACE

*A man's real possession is his memory. In nothing else is he rich, in nothing else is he poor.*
—ALEXANDER SMITH

*Tell me, I'll forget. Show me, I may remember. But involve me and I'll understand.*    —CHINESE PROVERB

*The true art of memory is the art of attention.*
—SAMUEL JOHNSON

*The memory represents to us not what we choose but what it pleases.*    —MONTAIGNE

S, the Russian wizard whose story was told in Chapter 2, went about memorizing in his own way. But systems like his to increase the power of memory have been used for thousands of years. From the earliest to the latest, these systems rely on similar means. They construct bold and original images; they call for intense concentration at the moment of memorization; they insist on steady practice; and they assume a powerful desire to improve the memory.

Some memory trainers make the doubtful claim that anyone can develop fabulous recall. Would S have performed so stunningly without some special gift of nature? Luria said that the mental capacity of S was unique:

> There is no question that S's exceptional memory was an innate characteristic, an element of his in-

dividuality, and that the techniques he used were merely superimposed on an existing structure and did not "simulate" it with devices other than those which were natural to it.

So although systems and methods for improving memory always appeal to people, it's not likely that the experts will help you to a "perfect memory." Memory-training programs that show promise usually apply recent research on learning in an attempt to improve your speed of learning and your ability to retain what you learn.

Let's look back to earlier times when such ideas were developed. The story of Matteo Ricci and his "memory palace" is a good starting point. Ricci was an Italian Jesuit who entered China in 1583 to do missionary work. It was the beginning of an astonishing adventure that lasted twenty-seven years, until his death. China at that time was a closed country. The rulers considered China to be the center of the world, the only source of civilization. It had no need of foreigners and rarely allowed them in. But, using the familiar tools of bribery, gifts, and other pressures, a few Italian Jesuits worked their way in. They came as scholars, making no mention of Christianity at first. They managed to win some acceptance among the educated classes. Ricci, a brilliant man, hoped to be received by the Emperor of China, to convert him first, then all the dignitaries, and through them the whole vast empire. He lived in various provincial cities and finally won permission to settle in Peking. He led an adventurous life and suffered many hardships. But he mastered the language, became friendly with Chinese officials and scholars, learned much about their culture from them, and in turn brought them news of Western science.

He worked in tremendous isolation. Sometimes it took seventeen years for a letter from Europe to reach him. Usually it took at least three years. Most of his library he carried in his head, for he had a prodigious memory. It was the product of training in the Jesuit colleges of Italy. They applied a system of memory methods that went back to the first century B.C. It was a system scholars used until cheap printing made it much easier to find what they needed to know in readily available books.

The Catholic teachers saw a mnemonic system as a means "to remember heaven and hell." Their idea explains much about the use of images in religious paintings by such artists as Giotto (c. 1266–c. 1337) as well as by the poet Dante (1265–1321) in his *Inferno*. In a book written in the 1400s to sharpen Christian devotion in girls, the girls were urged to give to characters in the Bible, including Jesus, the faces of friends, so that they could be fixed in their memories, and then to place these figures in their own mental Jerusalem, patterning it on their own town. Thus, when alone in her room, each girl could relive the Bible story in her mind, calling up the familiar faces as she moved them through Jerusalem.

In Shakespeare's time, it was the usual thing to

know something about how to use memory and how to strengthen it. In his play *Hamlet*, Shakespeare has Ophelia cry, "There's rosemary, that's for remembrance; pray you, love, remember." She says that to her brother Laertes, because she wants him never to forget that Hamlet has killed their father, Polonius, and to avenge that death. The herb rosemary, in many mnemonic booklets of the time, was said to be the best thing for strengthening the memory.

Ricci—of the same generation as Shakespeare—published a *Treatise on the Mnemonic Arts* in China. He guessed that this subject would attract the young Chinese who needed to memorize the classics to pass the examinations that assured a post in the government. The Chinese mandarins wanted their sons to pass, of course, and they welcomed a book in the Chinese language that would teach them his method.

The method depended upon the use of real or imaginary buildings, "memory palaces," filled in your mind with images linked to what you wanted to remember. You pictured in your mind successive rooms and apartments, housing images that could represent different types of knowledge—history, anatomy, geology. . . . It was meant to be a kind of memory retrieval system, one you could keep adding to.

It seems impossibly elaborate and complex to us, and it struck some of the young Chinese the same way. As one of them said of Ricci's methods, "One has to have a remarkably fine memory to make any use of them." Even scholars of the Renaissance era doubted their usefulness. Francis Bacon dismissed memory palaces as of no more account than "the tricks of tumblers."

At the root of Ricci's method was the idea of forming a strong association. This is common to almost all memory techniques. The ancient Greeks and Romans had the same approach. They tied what they wanted to remember to a particular, familiar place. It might be one's own house, with each room in it, or each object in it, made into a standard list of locations. Each item to be remembered would be imagined as linked to a specific location. So you only had to go back in your mind and think of the first location to get the first item you wished to recall, and then the second place, and so on. Roman orators used this system to memorize their speeches.

Such devices, as we saw earlier, are called "mnemonics." A mnemonic can be any method that helps you to remember something. Before printing was invented and books became easily available, the memory of people had to carry knowledge from place to place and from generation to generation.

The handwritten journal of Jasper Danckaerts, a Dutchman who traveled to New York in 1679, tells how the local Indians, without writing, relied on memory to pass the contents of treaties and contracts down through the generations. As the Indians negotiated with the white settlers for land sales, for each article of an agreement taken up, one of the Indians would hold a different shell in his hand. When agreement was reached, the specific meaning of that shell-marker was repeated in words.

Danckaerts's journal goes on to note of the Indians: "As they can neither read nor write, they are gifted with a powerful memory. After the conclusion of the matter, all the children who have the ability to understand and remember it are called together, and then they are told by their fathers, sachems, or chiefs how they entered into such a contract with these parties. [The children] are commanded to remember this treaty and to plant each article in particular in their memory." The shells were tied together with string, put in a bag, and hung in the house of the Indian chief. He adds that the young people were warned to preserve the memory "faithfully so that they may not become treaty-breakers, which is an abomination" to the Indians, he said.

When everyone relies on memory, the skill is developed and taught. The first specialist in mnemonics whose name has come down to us was the Greek poet Simonides (c. 556–468 B.C.). The story goes that while at a banquet in a rich man's house, Simonides was called outside. A moment later, the roof of the banquet hall collapsed, crushing beyond recognition the guests at the big table. When relatives came for the bodies, they could not identify them. Simonides was able to tell who each mangled guest was. He did this by recalling where each of them had sat. Then he identified by place each of the bodies. That experience led him to invent the classic system of memory that Ricci taught the Chinese two thousand years later.

Simonides' system prevailed in Europe for many centuries. It was based on the two simple ideas of place and image.

Anyone who could display a special talent for memory became a celebrity. Remember, in the ancient world, printing was unknown. There was no paper on which to take notes or write out lectures and speeches. Naturally, then, poet and priest, singer and actor, doctor and lawyer needed a highly developed memory to carry out their functions. Earlier, it was noted that the *Iliad* and the *Odyssey* were preserved by word of mouth. Of course, before the spread of printing, writing was the means to pass on information, but manuscripts were expensive to produce, few in number, hard to read, and hard to preserve. So people still relied mostly on memory. Laws were stored in the community memory before they entered the lawbooks. Religious services, repeated regularly, fixed ritual and liturgy in the minds of the congregation. Before there were printed textbooks, scholars often passed on their learning through thousands of lines of rhymed verse. Copied out by hand, they later became the stuff of textbooks. Manuscript handbooks on memory went through many editions and were widely translated.

It was the German Johannes Gutenberg (c. 1400–1468) whose invention of printing with movable type became the substitute for memory. Books in manuscript form had been a crutch for the memory of a tiny number of educated people. But the printed book—

more accurate, more readable, more portable, and far more widely distributed—removed the need to store all knowledge in your own head.

Both memory and manuscript books lost out to printing. Printed books had numbered pages and were soon provided with indexes. You could use the alphabetic index at the back of a book to find the information you needed. Why bother with elaborate systems of memory recall? No wonder they were often dismissed as not worth the trouble. The common needs for memory were no longer as vital as in the days before printing. Memory itself was put down by some. The French essayist Montaigne said in 1580 that "a good memory is generally joined to a weak judgment." And "nothing is more common," someone added, "than a fool with a strong memory."

The historian of early memory systems, Frances A. Yates, herself takes the commonsense view "that all these places and images would only bury under a heap of rubble whatever little one does remember naturally." She thinks the advocates of such systems, such as Cicero, must have had "a fantastically acute visual memory."

Still, almost as soon as printing was invented, a memory textbook was written by Peter of Ravenna and published in Italy in 1491. It was widely translated and went through many editions. What made it enormously popular was that it applied mnemonics to the everyday world of business. The man with a trained memory would do better in a competitive world, Peter promised. Never mind remembering hell: Now you could apply Peter's methods to getting on right here on earth.

Memorization is still an essential part of the learning process. And learning by rote, by constant repetition till the material is lodged securely in memory, continues to be used. Mnemonic devices play their part. These unusual tricks or combinations force you to remember; they work as attention grabbers. Sometimes making up a ditty or poem does it. Thus, to recall the number of days in each month: "Thirty days hath September / April, June, and November. . . ." The rhymes and the beat give instant recall of the needed facts.

In music, the notes on the treble staff are E, G, B, D, and F. To make them stick in the head in the right order, pupils learn the line "Every Good Boy Deserves Fudge."

Psychology textbooks discuss various techniques of learning. Besides mnemonic devices, they take up what's called "principle learning"; that means, to acquire general principles that can be applied to many instances of what you are learning. An illustration: You are asked to memorize a series of numbers—574, 575, 579, 583, 584, 588, 592, 593. Once you see the relationship between these numbers, you need only memorize the first number. The principle is, add 1, add 4, add 4, then 1, then 4, then 4, then 1, and so on. You could now reel off dozens of numbers in this sequence. To learn them by rote would be much harder and take much longer.

Another aid to learning is called "consolidation theory." This calls for you to study something, then rest. The theory claims that the memory storage system needs time for the material learned to consolidate, or set. So if you would take frequent short breaks during study, rather than try to learn a great deal at one time, you'd do better. There's no fixed rule for such periods of rest. A good idea is to take a break whenever you feel your attention wandering.

If you think back to Chapter 3, where long- and short-term memory are discussed, you'll see how the consolidation theory fits in. It's based on the belief that long-term memory needs enough time for its "circuits" to come together to form the memory. Without periods of rest, too much material would come in and fire other circuits that might interfere with the original learning—that is, not allow it to "set."

Another means of learning, disagreeable but effective, is recitation—no, not public performance, but repeating silently to yourself what you want to learn. The method is to read a paragraph or so of the material and then recite in your own words what you've just read. It focuses the attention and makes you stick with the stuff. If you go on reading steadily, without stopping for silent recitation, you tend to take in too much, and it competes for a place in your long-term memory.

This is not literal, or verbatim, memorizing. That is done when faithfulness to a particular text is desired. You couldn't sing "The Star-Spangled Banner" without using the exact words. Otherwise, it isn't the national anthem. We use literal recall often in our lives—

to learn the Preamble to the Constitution ("We, the people of the United States") or Hamlet's soliloquy ("To be, or not to be: that is the question") or "Now I lay me down to sleep . . ."

When I was young, everyone in our class had to learn by heart a poem to fire our patriotism:

> Then up spake brave Horatius,
> The keeper of the gate:
> "To every man upon the earth
> Death cometh soon or late.
> And how can man die better
> Than facing fearful odds
> For the ashes of his fathers
> And the temples of his gods?"

Nor will I ever forget the words of the great speech Lincoln gave at Gettysburg in the middle of the Civil War: "Fourscore and seven years ago . . ."

When given free choice of a poem to memorize and perform in the school auditorium, I picked Kipling's pounding rhythmic chant:

> (Boots—boots—boots—boots—
>           moving' up and down
>                         again!)
> There's no discharge in the war!

Of course, there are many other ways to aid memory. Some of these you've probably dreamed up yourself. A common device is to write down a list of things you have to do, and then look at it routinely to remind yourself of what's to be done next. (It doesn't work if you forget to take the list with you or to look at it!) Then there are external clues you plant to prod your memory. You put the overdue library book at the front door so you'll see it on the way out and return it. You place the bottle of multivitamins in the bathroom next to your toothbrush so you'll take one after you brush your teeth. You leave your tennis racket on the table next to the phone so you'll remember to call your partner for that date to play.

Shopping lists, alarm clocks or electric timers, keeping notebooks, phone number books or birthday books, are the kinds of memory aids many of us use. Some people rely on internal memory aids. For instance, when shopping without a written list, they remember the total number of things to be bought as well as what the items are. They might forget an item or two, but if they recall the number, they will jostle their memory till they find the items they need to fill out the list. Another method is to imagine what was in the refrigerator the last time you looked in it, and then shop for what's needed to fill the gaps.

Or there's the ancient trick of tying a string around your finger to remember—what? To buy string?

# CHAPTER VIII

# TOSCANINI AND BLIND TOM

*Man does not consist of memory alone. . . . He has feeling, will, sensibilities, moral being . . . matters of which neuropsychology cannot speak.*    —A. R. LURIA

*How·vast a memory has Love!*    —ALEXANDER POPE

*A man's memory may almost become the art of continually varying and misrepresenting his past, according to his interests in the present.*
    —GEORGE SANTAYANA

How do musicians memorize a score? Actors, a part? Dancers, the choreography?

Let's begin with musicians. Earlier we referred to Toscanini's fabulous memory. His was an extraordinary gift, but numbers of others have shared it to some degree. At the opposite pole from the highly trained Toscanini was the uneducated and sightless slave child Thomas Bethune, born in Georgia in 1849. He gave early evidence of unusual sensitivity to sound. He delighted in sounds, whether the soft breathings of a flute or the harsh grating of a corn sheller. At four, he heard music played on a piano for the first time, sat down at the keyboard, and played the piece through from memory.

The young prodigy was encouraged by whites, and in youth was able to tour America and Europe, giving concerts of music by such composers as Bach, Beethoven, and Mendelssohn. They were programs all learned from auditory memory. One of his showmanly feats was to have people from the audience come up to the platform and play some new pieces while he sat apart listening. On one hearing, he repeated what was played to him. At the height of his career, it was reported that he could play from memory seven thousand pieces. Several of the leading musicians of his day testified to his unusual ability.

Mozart offers another example of extraordinary feats of memory. When he was twelve, he heard the *Miserere* of Gregorio Allegri in the Papal Chapel in Rome. It was considered the exclusive property of the Vatican Choir, and no one was allowed to copy it. But Mozart went home after the performance and wrote it down from memory. It was no small accomplishment: The work was written partly for four- and partly for five-voice chorus and with a nine-voice finale.

The French composer Camille Saint-Saëns, who heard performances of Wagner's operas in Paris, could play all those scores from memory. He could also reproduce their several parts, whether they were leading or minor themes. Wagner himself marveled at this great gift.

The conductor Eugene Ormandy was catapulted into that career by his extraordinary memory. As a young violinist from Hungary, he got work in the orchestra of a Broadway movie theater. This was in the days when a live musical performance was added to the feature film. One night the conductor was suddenly taken ill, and Ormandy, with no notice, was asked to take his place. He put down his violin, went up to the podium, and, never having held a baton before, conducted Tchaikovsky's Fourth Symphony from memory.

That feat launched him on a new career. Thereafter, he continued to conduct entirely without a score, learning a new symphony or concerto in a day or two. Of course, there are conductors just as distinguished who do not rely on a phenomenal musical memory. The advantage of memory, it is said, is that it allows a conductor to communicate through his eyes with every musician in the orchestra. And that may help heighten or intensify the performance.

Remote from concert hall performance is the account of black freedom fighters sentenced by the white South African government to imprisonment on Robben Island off Cape Town. One of them, Joe Seremane, proudly recalled a jazz combo in which he played in the prison. The warden refused to let them have instruments, but that did not stop their music making. They did bop scatting by voice. Each man's voice played like two or three instruments, drawing on fantastic memory of the music, and combining with the other instrumental voices.

Of course, to memorize a long and complex piece of music—an opera or symphony—must be immensely hard. Some musicians go about it by first breaking the composition down into meaningful parts. They find this better than to start with the first measure and work through to the last. One opera conductor, for instance, says he first seeks an overall view of the opera. Then he studies the order of the acts, and the scenes within each act. With its dramatic structure clearly in mind, he starts to learn the music itself, one scene after the other, and measure by measure. Because he has the whole shape in mind, he knows where he is at every point. But if one lacks a natural musical memory, or if it is unreliable, faulty, flighty, is there anything to be done to improve it? People like Toscanini or Ormandy never studied memorizing as such. Probably most of us nonmusicians assume memorizing to be an ingredient of a musician's talent, to be taken for granted.

If memorizing is not the easiest thing to do, musicians can be trained to do it by various methods. To summarize but one such teacher's methods: She speaks of three separate phases of "memory control"— reflex action, auditory images, and visual images.

For an instrumentalist, reflex action—"learning a piece in the fingers"—is the first and most natural source of memory, something essential to good performance. But this is treacherous and uncertain, she adds, because the reflexes are so easily interfered with. A slight noise, a sudden movement across the line of vision, a stray thought, may so interrupt the reflexes that the performer has no idea where he is in the piece. He can only go back to begin again at some point he can think of to start him on the road again. Think of what's involved in memorizing a piano sonata. A single such piece by Chopin may last twenty minutes and require the playing of ten thousand notes. For some pieces the pianist must play perhaps twenty-five notes per second for many minutes. If the performer even questions his mind as to what comes next, the reflexes are interfered with and may refuse to go on. So the nervous system makes the reflex the least reliable of memory resources. Yet it can't be dispensed with, for it's what carries along the performer's motions, "making them smooth, easy, flowing, free." It must be used, but together with the mental activity that makes the motions safe.

For those whose mind works readily in auditory images, the memorizing of music comes more easily. Probably you can remember a simple tune. The musician, however, must think the complex sounds of chords and involved harmonic structure and must hear them in his mind when "remembering" a piece of music. Most musicians quickly store in their minds the sound memory of music often repeated. Those who can readily transfer that to notes on the instrument memorize so easily they don't know how they do it.

More people seem to think in visual rather than auditory images. And for these people, musical memorizing needs steady training. In the case of instrumentalists, the visual images are of two sorts: how the image of the music looks on the score, and how it looks on the instrument. The way it looks on the instrument, says one teacher, "comes more or less easily along with the training of the reflex motions. Repeated practice of a passage will bring at the same time a habit of action and a sense of the appearance of the hands on the instrument."

The would-be musician is warned that learning to memorize a piece and playing it without lapse of memory—thinking the notes, seeing them on the mind and on the instrument—is only the first stage of the work of mastering a composition. It simply helps free the mind of the effort to recall. To re-create the music, with its emotions, moods, atmosphere, and meaning, comes next and is far more important.

What about actors? How do they learn their lines for a play or a film or a TV performance? And does the memorizing of a part hang on in the mind? The comic actor Milton Berle began performing in a Charlie Chaplin film as far back as 1914, when he was a little child. He became the first great TV star in a comedy series in 1948, when the new medium became a national craze and Berle was called "Mr. Television." The gags flowed out of him in an endless stream. He had one ready for any situation. Recently Berle said he had set up a computer filing system with cross-references for all his jokes and boasted of programming over 6 million of them. "But," he added, pointing to his head, "I've got 150,000 up here."

Another veteran actor and entertainer, the Englishman Stanley Holloway, talked about his career shortly before his death at the age of ninety-one. "I have had a very good memory," he said. "I remember at school playing in Shakespeare's *Henry the Eighth*. I played Wolsey, and I have never looked at it from that day to this, but I can go through Wolsey's speech: 'Farewell! a long farewell. . . . ' I could go through the whole speech today, and I have never seen it since I was about twelve or thirteen. But that is what memory does. It fools you because you think you remember things and suddenly it is gone."

Holloway's memory loss was patchy. As for most people, it varied according to his interests and preoccupations of the moment.

A specialist in the psychology of memory observes that when experienced actors set out to master a new role, they don't begin by memorizing the part. Instead, they study the role to understand the character and to find a pattern of meanings in the words and actions. As they search for the meaning, they memorize the part as a by-product of that search.

I confirmed this when I interviewed several professional actors. They agreed that, when cast in a play, actors don't come to the first rehearsal with their lines memorized. Typically, the director sits down with the cast for one or two readings of the play. Over the next few days, the cast members get to know one another and, with script in hand, feel their way into their own part and its relationship to the other characters. They look for behavioral patterns beneath the dialogue. As they move into active rehearsal, they get to know what they're doing and what their character wants or expects from the other characters. Finally the lines— which they've read many times from the script—lodge firmly in the memory and appear to come naturally.

"You find the voice of your character," as one actress put it, and "what she has to say flows from your understanding of her, your feeling for her." She said she couldn't imagine sitting down before rehearsals begin to memorize the whole part by rote. "Perhaps some actors do it that way, but very few, I think."

"To learn a part by rote, before rehearsals," said another actor, "would be to memorize it in a vacuum." He masters his part during rehearsals. With pencil in hand, he goes over his script to break it down into what he calls "beats": that is, the arc of a speech or a scene that follows a thought process to its end, or to where it is redirected by what another character does or says. He circles key words and underlines nouns and verb action. "It's learning my part in chunks," he said.

Some actors are gifted with photographic memory. They need only look over the script to have their part groove itself into the mind. But not many are so blessed. Most start with an average memory; the more acting they do, the better developed their memory may become. This doesn't mean that a part, once learned, will stick forever. After playing a leading role on Broadway for two years, said one actress, "I found that a week after the play closed, I couldn't remember a line." Quite unlike Stanley Holloway.

A number of talented actors play roles in television soap operas. Unlike a stage play, where the same lines are called for in every performance, each day's episode requires new dialogue. Some soap opera directors will permit certain actors to paraphrase their lines. As one actor told me, he reads over his part the night before the next day's episode is to be videotaped, and comes into the studio with a firm grasp of what each of his scenes is about. Then, instead of giving the lines as written, he paraphrases the script, making many of the words his own. "I would never do this with Chekhov or Tennessee Williams," he said, "but in a soap opera? The lines are hardly immortal."

And dancers? "There are basically two ways ballet dancers learn the choreography," said a woman who is a principal dancer with the American Ballet Theatre. "One is to watch the steps as the choreographer goes through them, observing his gestures and movements, punctuated by his comments. I could never memorize my part in a ballet that way—through the eye only. I have to do each step along with the choreographer, as he does it, and standing behind him. If I stood facing him, it would be a mirror image, with his left my right, and so on. It is easier to place myself behind, so that his right is my right, his left my left."

For the dance, music is an essential part of performance. Its rhythms and patterns reinforce mastering the movement of the body. The dancer said, "I begin to learn my role by going over it in my mind—first I do this, then I do that, I take so many steps in this direction, then turn, pirouette, etc., etc. This while listening to the music on a tape or recording. Sometimes I lay out the plan on the floor at home for the space I will dance in on stage."

At this point, her mind is consciously memorizing

the choreography, "but after constant rehearsing of the movements, another level of the brain takes over—call it kinesthetic memory. The body itself seems to have mastered the role. It is something like learning to ride a bicycle or swim or skate. I don't have to think what to do next. There's the music playing and my body moves in the learned response to it."

A modern dancer and choreographer says that she has always found it hard to memorize a dance, her own or another's. She must keep rehearsing steadily until the body takes it up without mental strain. When conceiving a new dance, she makes many notes as she goes along, developing new ideas, new movements, and new patterns, using her own shorthand for the purpose. She also uses videotape or film to record the phases of her choreography and to remind herself of what's been done. Luckily, she can rely on one or two dancers in her own group who have marvelous recall of even the smallest details of a dance. Her own memory fails that test. When she sees the title of a dance she created years ago, she cannot rememer how it went. But some small clue—a costume, a setting, a single movement—may release the memory, and it rushes back in.

When choreographers retire or die, how are the dances they have conceived passed on to others? If not by someone who learned directly from the creator, then it is by a dance notation system such as Labanotation. It was developed by Rudolf Laban in the 1920s. It records completely and accurately, for study or reconstruction, the work of such choreographers as George

Balanchine or Martha Graham. It has had the same effect on ballet and the dance as the perfection of music notation in the Renaissance had on the development of that art. Choreographers need not rely on human memory to see their work passed on. Labanotation, said Balanchine, "records the structure of a dance, revealing with perfect clarity each of the specific movements of each performer."

Relatively few dancers master the complex method. But there is a Dance Notation Bureau in New York City whose trained staff can record choreography by this method, and use it to teach others how to perform a dance. In such cases, as with the performance of music from a written score, or a play from a script, it is the artist who must interpret the dance to convey its unique quality to the audience.

# CHAPTER IX

# IS THE COMPUTER AS GOOD?

---

*A liar ought to have a good memory.*      —APULEIUS

*Reminiscences make one feel so deliciously aged and sad.*      —GEORGE BERNARD SHAW

*A good memory is generally joined to a weak judgment.*      —MONTAIGNE

*Our memories are card indexes consulted, and then put back in disorder by authorities whom we do not control.*      —CYRIL CONNOLLY

What about the memory of a computer? How good is it, and how does it compare with human memory?

Back in 1945, when the computer was new and primitive, it could store ten words in memory. In 1955, the capacity was a small book. In 1964, it was the whole set of an encyclopedia; in 1975, a million-volume library. And in the 1990s?

The second most important feature of a computer is its incredible memory. (The first is the incredible speed with which it recalls items from its memory.) It has enormous capacity to store and to recall indefinitely what has been programmed into it.

Tiny memory chips now manipulate data in electronic equipment of all sorts, from computers to videocassette recorders. In the late 1970s, memory chips could store about 16,000 pieces of information. New chips, called the megabit RAM (the initials stand for

Random Access Memory), were developed with four times that storage capacity. They pack more than one million transistors in the space that until then held only 250,000.

Today's robots used in manufacturing have elements built in that enable the robot to solve its own problems to some extent. Robots run on predetermined programs. For example, if two gears in an oil pump don't fit together after a certain number of tries, the robot goes into a problem mode and stops operating until a human attendant makes a correction. With artificial intelligence programming, a robot facing an obstacle will try different solutions to a problem, at first probably at random. But as its random attempts bring some successes, these are stored in the control computer's memory. And when the same obstacles are met again, the robot "remembers" the solution and tries that first.

Very impressive, but, as the mathematician John Kemeny has pointed out, it took the development of the computer "to show just how remarkably good human memory is." The human memory still exceeds that of the best computer today. True, it is much slower in its working, but it is still remarkably efficient. How it does it is as yet something of a mystery; we saw that in earlier chapters on memory research. Whatever the human processes of memory may be, no one has duplicated them in a computer.

The power of a high-speed computer is realized through a variety of procedures for which it is programmed. The human mind figures out what it wants the computer to do and instructs it on how to do it. A program can be a few instructions or hundreds of thousands; it depends on the complexity of the task. It takes much time and great effort for humans to instruct the computer. But once the program has been set, the computer can be repeated endlessly; that is, unless poor maintenance or worn-out parts interfere.

Miniaturization and new technology, such as laser beams, are making computer memory vastly greater than anything achieved before. Then why bother with the human memory? Because we still cannot do without it—either because we don't know how to accomplish the task with the computer alone, or because the human mind has certain talents the computer does not have. This goes even with mathematical calculation, which the computer was originally designed to do. The living mathematician can recognize subtle patterns that take him to shortcuts; the computer is not yet able to do that. It seems to be a talent that it is not suited for.

Nor is it adaptable for many other mysterious processes of association the human memory demonstrates all the time. As Dr. Kemeny puts it:

> How does one associate a phrase in a book with a conversation held ten years ago? How does one associate a smell with a childhood memory? How, in trying to solve a problem, do we pull out three unrelated memories going back to different peri-

ods in our life to come up with a new approach to
the solution? And how do we sift through hope-
lessly large amounts of information presented to
us daily by our senses and retain just the most rel-
evant facts?

Kemeny adds that "while computers are magnifi-
cent beasts, they are in many respects very stupid."
They have no judgment or common sense. They can
get into hopeless tangles and be unable to try a new
approach. While ways of checking their work are now
built in, the computer ultimately relies on the human
mind to do the evaluation.

Or take intuition and creativity. Humans have these
indefinable gifts. No machine has them. The computer
can make a thousand passes at a problem while the
human mind tries a dozen. But chances are that the
intuitive guess of the human will find the solution
while the computer fails.

So it seems best for humans to work in harmony
with the computer. They can design better and better
computers and better ways to program them. They can
decide how best to use them. They can set the goals
and instruct the computer on how to reach them. And
they can watch the computer at work and evaluate the
results.

The human mind is often compared to what the
computer does: information processing. The mind is
said to be filled with cognitive devices of various
kinds. They process input that comes in from the envi-

ronment and produce a response or output. The brain
is seen as a wonderfully effective information processing system. It transforms the incoming information a
little or a lot, and causes it to stay in the memory any-
where from briefly (short-term memory) to permanently (long-term memory). It works not as a struc-
tured mechanism but rather as a series of processes.
(Specialists in memory do not agree on what those processes are or how they operate.)

The computer, of course, is not made up of living
cells, but of semiconductors, wires, and other electronic devices. Are computer hardware and the brain's
neuron network essentially the same? Not at all, but
the difference, say some experts in artificial intelligence, is not significant. Most cognitive scientists disagree. They say the functions of intelligence carried on
by the computer are not the same as human thought.
They may try to reach the same goals, but they take
very different paths. Each has advantages and also lim-
itations. The computer can do some tasks much better
than the human mind, but it is far from being able to
imitate the complex and subtle processes of a human
mind. You cannot look to the computer to see how the
mind works.

One of the leading computer scientists, Claude
Shannon, observed that the behavior of ants is marvelous: "They're able to survive and live in this very
hostile environment we have, and reproduce and eat
and do everything they have to. And they have only a
few hundred nerve cells in them. It seems utterly in-

credible," he said, because if he had to do that with the same limited equipment, he really couldn't.

The modern computer is a complex instrument, but its components and method of operating are basically simple. In contrast, the human brain structure is incredibly complex, and so is the way it works. Even a very simple animal's brain operates in a far more complex way than does a computer. Even in what seems the simplest thing to us—the ability of the brain to recognize a face in a fraction of a second—the computer cannot compete, for no machine can do that.

One final point about the computer: It works to carry out a goal set by those who made the machine. Even a computer that can improve its own program is unable to set a new goal for itself. The human brain can do that. The machine has no means of doing it, and no reason to do it. Unlike the human mind, it has no consciousness. We can think and can perceive ourselves thinking. No computer is able to do that. And most experts doubt that any machine could ever do it.

CHAPTER    X

# WHAT HAPPENED TO HISTORY

---

*The struggle of man against power is the struggle of memory against forgetting.*    —MILAN KUNDERA

*The opposite of history is not myth. The opposite of history is forgetfulness.*    —ELIE WIESEL

*In the United States of Amnesia, we keep having to reinvent everything from scratch.*
    —JOSEPH FEATHERSTONE

*A good memory is needed after one has lied.*
    —CORNEILLE

A Chinese proverb says: "To understand a man you must know his memories. The same is true of a nation."

Memory: It is our one direct link with the past. What we are is the result of the past. The past shapes the present. The present is what we build upon to create the future. To forget about the past is to betray it, and therefore to spoil the present and the future.

How do we know the past? We can speak reliably about recent events we ourselves have experienced. About other events we can learn from family, friends, and neighbors. In either case, we find out through recall that puts us in touch with the events we want to know about. For the traditions of our society, we turn to grandparents and the transmitted recollections of the generations before them. These, too, are based upon memory, like our own personal recollections.

Those traditions are the elements of experience that one generation after another chooses to hand down, deepening the pool of collective memory.

Before written history there was legend. For thousands of years before writing was invented, people's knowledge of the past came from what the wisest elders of the community said. Those stories that were trusted were repeated and preserved, as a treasure-house of memory. They testified to the past. Making up the collective memory of ancestors, they became the history of early societies.

Time passing was measured by the names of ancestors. Genealogy was not a matter of personal pride or curiousity then; it was a social necessity. It linked the people of the present to those who came before. It was a lifeline to beginnings. That is why the Bible is so rich in genealogy. And that is why tribes without written records have good reason to develop the power of memory. Tribal elders keep track of history by carefully storing it in memory and passing it on, with additions, to the oncoming generations. On ceremonial occasions, they meet to chant together the legends of the tribe and thus fix them ever more firmly in the mind. Earlier, we noted the power of bards to memorize traditional epic poems that preserved the community's chronicles. Such chronicles of African tribes serve the same purpose as the *Iliad* and the *Odyssey*. The bards in such societies are the historians of their people. Only memory, in the days before scrolls and books, kept their stories alive.

Today, of course, any historian learns vastly more about his subject than the bards of the preliterate societies. He holds it in memory in the form of his notes and through the articles and books and other documents where the details are stored. What he needs to remember is chiefly his retrieval system. Most of the material is not in his head but in those files, where it won't fade away.

History as something recorded about the past goes back to the great empires of the Middle East. They set down in stone, long before 3000 B.C., the names of rulers and the wars of their dynasties. The earliest relic of that ancient time is a fragment of hard black diorite stone on which was inscribed the names of the first Egyptian kings. Later monuments recorded richer details of the country's history. But like "official history" in any time, their aim was more to glorify the people in power than to tell the truth.

Recorded history, then, goes back at most to only five thousand years before our time. It's important to realize that, for most of that time, the pace of social, economic, and political change was much slower than today. People for a great many centuries lived much as their ancestors had done. They knew there were good times and bad, that monarchies rose and fell, but life was much the same over the long sweep of time. So they didn't think of historical development in the way we think of it now. Change! Rapid, inevitable, often frightening. Earlier times never felt that. I myself was born when the automobile and the airplane were primitive and rarely seen, and now men fly to the moon. All this has happened in much less than a century.

But my purpose here is not to provide a history of history. It is, rather, to point to the role of memory in history, both personal and collective. The historian is the creator and custodian of the memory of civilizations. A civilization without memory is no longer civilized. It loses its identity. If it doesn't know what it is and where it comes from, it has no purpose. Without purpose, it withers and dies.

What we think of our government is shaped by what the historian has told us as much as by our experience of the way that government functions. We look to Washington for certain things: justice, equality, freedom. We have certain expectations of it when it comes to protecting and improving the material welfare of our lives, because of our sense of what is has done in the past, and what it stands for. What the government does now or fails to do to meet our expectations may fulfill those hopes or disappoint them. The result is sometimes a new view of the outcome or direction of history.

Washington is not some given thing, an object, or a cluster of institutions that exists outside time, independent of anything else. It is an ever-changing structure of government molded by the conflict of forces and people in the past and influenced by the same elements today. Our understanding of it, our attitude toward it, is shaped by memory of the past, memory transmitted by the historian.

Yet, as the political columnist James Reston says, "Even in Washington history is a parade of forgotten memories." The study of history is no longer required in most high schools, and in many states even the teachers of history have little or no serious training in the subject.

A Secretary of Education, William J. Bennett, was alarmed by that situation in 1985:

> The present decline in the status of history in our schools is very serious. . . . We cannot hope that our students will know why the world got into its present situation—or even what that situation is—if they know so little of the events that came before them.

And Reston adds that, with history so neglected, "we shouldn't be surprised if the people elect members of the Congress and even Presidents who share their shaky knowledge or even ignorance of the history of the world."

When history *is* taught in the schools, it is often with the help of textbooks that treat the past very gingerly. "The right to search for truth implies also a duty," wrote Albert Einstein. "One must not conceal any part of what one has recognized to be true."

But when Frances Fitzgerald analyzed American history textbooks not long ago, she found that controversial ideas were often left out. Liberal and radical figures and trends were shunned. The textbooks tiptoed around all ideas, in fact, including those of the nation's heroes. What Thomas Jefferson or Martin Luther King, Jr., thought and did was either ignored or so watered down as to be meaningless. So, too, were the ideas and actions of people such as Senator Joseph McCarthy or Adolf Hitler. The heroes were deflated and the villains laundered—all with an eye to being politically safe, beyond criticism or reproach. Such versions of our collective memory confuse basic issues and values. History is made mush.

Stirred into the mush are dishonesty and deception and, yes, even betrayal. Is this true only of our own treatment of our past? Of course not. The Nigerian writer Wole Soyinka has called for a stark emphasis on "the enemy within"—that is, on what is wrong with the elements in his own society that has caused the failure of the colonial revolution to fulfill its promise: "The repetitive experience of betrayal, of failures, in Africa today surrounds us in every event." That is why, he went on, "a writer cannot lie to the people."

In another part of the continent, the country of South Africa, a black majority has been struggling for many years for freedom and equality. The white minority in power has used every weapon at its command, including banishment, prison sentences, and murder, to maintain its system of apartheid. It is a system of discriminatory racial legislation. By law, it denies human, political, and economic rights to its citizens purely on the basis of race. Its advocates claim that it provides for the separate but parallel development of people whose skins are of a different color. But the United Nations General Assembly has declared apartheid to be "a crime against humanity."

Falsifying memory is one major means the ruling regime in South Africa uses to maintain itself in power. The textbooks it provides the schools with grossly distort the past in order to justify apartheid. The claims the goverment makes about its system have nothing to do with apartheid's realities. The government, says the historian Leonard Thompson, has manufactured a history, or rather a mythology, to bolster its politics.

This kind of falsification of memory, of the past, is done almost everywhere, in different degree and with varying effect. In antidemocratic societies, history is always rewritten to suit the government's latest position. It happens even in democratic countries. What France remembers of the period during World War II, after the Germans defeated it and when the Nazis occupied part of the country, is an example.

What some hope is forgotten is that numbers of French citizens thrived as informers in the hire of Gestapo chiefs such as Klaus Barbie, and that many French collaborated in carrying out Hitler's extermination of the Jews. The wartime chief of the Paris police, Jean Leguay, was responsible for deporting four thousand Jewish children to their death. After the war, he was pardoned and became a multimillionaire. The memory of that past is what many French people would prefer to keep buried. If the truth came to light, it might destroy the myth of a nation that united, gloriously, in resisting the Nazi yoke.

A seventeen-year-old, Arnaud de Bussac, cherishes his grandfather who was in the resistance and then in a concentration camp. "He is the crucible of our memory," he said. "He has forced us [his family] to remember the past, to a far greater degree than most of our generation. And one must remember in order not to start again; it is forgetfulness which could start another war."

In Japan, forgetfulness of the historic past has been commonplace. Only recently have Japanese tourists vacationing in Hawaii come to visit the monument of Pearl Harbor. There, on December 7, 1941, Japanese planes bombed the American fleet lying at anchor, bringing the United States into World War II. A plaque lists the 1,777 names of the American sailors who died there. In the harbor are the charred remains of the battleship *Arizona*, sunk that day long ago.

Pearl Harbor and the other Japanese actions in the war are not held firmly in mind by the Japanese. The schools teach only the chronology of the war, without any comment or judgment. The textbooks and teachers' guides do not encourage discussion about the lessons of the war, though they do stress the need for peace.

For Japan, the horror of Hiroshima and Nagasaki are far more overwhelming than Pearl Harbor. But a Japanese professor of history, Kiyoko Takeda, thinks it harmful for the nation not to confront the symbolic importance of Pearl Harbor and Japan's role as an aggressor. "In general," he says, "Japanese tend to forget the past, thinking that it can be washed away. But I always tell my students that recognizing what we have done in the past is a recognition of ourselves. By conducting a dialogue with our past, we are searching how to go forward."

One man who has dug back into his Japanese childhood is Kensuke Fukae. He remembers how a military spirit was bred in the schools and history books in Japan. It was helped by the creation of an actual Thought Police. The news was censored for "national security" reasons. Any dissenter, whether an editor or professor or politician, could be arrested as a Communist sympathizer. Every action of the government was justified on grounds of "national security."

What the end of all this would be, the world soon learned: death to millions of many nations in a terrible war that devastated Asia. Kensuke Fukae, now an American citizen, warns us:

> America, unlike Japan, has a strong tradition of dissent. This country was built on the right to challenge authority. Such a tradition was tragically absent in my homeland as I grew up; Americans should cherish it, for it is such rights that most merit their patriotic devotion. Our loyalty was to our leaders—America's must be to the Constitution.

The blotting out of collective memory was the rigid rule in most Latin American countries until recently. As the 1980s began, there were only three democracies on that continent. Today, many of the brutal regimes have been replaced by new governments struggling to restore democracy and to recover the true history of their people.

Under the repressive governments, kidnapping, torture, disappearances, and assassinations were commonplace. But violence against the physical body was made possible by a war against ideas that was just as deadly. The military juntas hounded writers, artists, teachers, and students, jailed them without charge, tortured them, killed them, or forced them into exile. Publishing houses were shut down, newspapers suppressed, books destroyed. Sociology and psychology were considered dangerous fields to enter because they call for analysis of what is going on in society or in the mind. Radio and television were directly controlled by the censors. Grade schools had to submit for approval lists of the books in their libraries. Total control of thought and expression was the goal. Those against the government had either to say nothing or to live in fear that anything they said or did would bring personal disaster.

For the victims of human rights abuses and their families and friends, it is hard to forget the past. Will such memories ever weaken? But many young people who have lived under dictatorships, according to sociologists, do not seem to be concerned about the past. Why? Because intellectual life is smothered under the pressures of strict censorship. Teachers, journalists, authors, playwrights, filmmakers, even songwriters are not allowed to speak the truth. So a whole generation of young people grows up without any living tie to government and politics. As terrible chapters in their country's history are unreeled, they sit by, blindfolded.

But there are voices that speak out against forgetting, voices from men and women who have lived through totalitarian horrors. One who was a soldier in Hitler's army became, long after, the President of West Germany. "We in the older generation," he said, "owe to young people, not the fulfillment of dreams, but honesty. Hitler's constant approach was to stir up prejudices, enmity, and hatred. What is asked of young people today is this: Do not let yourselves be forced into enmity and hatred of other people. Let us honor freedom. Let us work for peace. Let us respect the rule of law."

Richard von Weizsacker said these words on May 8, 1985, on the fortieth anniversary of the day Nazi Germany surrendered, bringing World War II to an end. "All of us, whether guilty or not, whether young or old, must accept the past," he said to his Parliament. "We are all affected by the consequences and liable for it. The young and old generations must and can help each other to understand why it is vital to keep alive the memories. . . . Anyone who closes his eyes to the past is blind to the present. Whoever refuses to remember the inhumanity is prone to new risks of infection. The Jewish nation remembers and will always remember. . . . If we for our part sought to forget what had occurred, instead of remembering it, this would not only be inhuman, we would also impinge upon the faith of the Jews who survived and destroy the basis of reconciliation."

President Weizsacker's speech stressed his country's need to confront the Nazi era—those dozen years of Nazi rule over Germany and then most of Europe. By the time Hitler's power was smashed, 50 million people were dead. They were from many different countries, including Hitler's Germany and our United States. Among the myriad slaughtered were the Jews: six million of them; two out of every three in Europe; one third of the world's Jews.

In recent years a film called *Shoah* has been screened in many theaters in America and abroad. (*Shoah*, in Hebrew, means "annihilation.") The long film is a voyage of discovery through memories of the Holocaust that bring back the past with a devastating power. The film is not a documentary composed of newsreel footage of the Holocaust and taken from the archives. Instead, it gives us the faces and words of witnesses today, men and women who were victims and survived, or who were Nazis who helped run the death camps, or Polish people who lived close by the camps planted on their countryside. Claude Lanzmann, the French maker of the film, does not use images recorded in the past. Those would put the past at a safe remove. He chose instead to gather relentlessly the details from the men and woman whose remembering restores the terrible experience they witnessed. The nine and a half hours of film add their strength to one of the most documented tragedies of history.

Using memory, Lanzmann succeeded in eliminating

the distance between past and present. He wanted, he said, "to aid the human conscience to never forget, to never accustom itself to the perversity of racism and its monstrous capacities for destruction."

Yet there are those who would forget history or, still worse, deny it. Former high-ranking officers in Hitler's Gestapo have publicly denied that there ever were death camps and gas chambers. They said all such stories had been created by propagandists. A great many others, including some historians, have said quite simply that six million Jews murdered in the Holocaust is a lie. It never happened. When the facts are produced, they will not believe them. They say such things never happened. They would like to undo the Holocaust by weakening the tenacity of memory. The aim is to bury the truth and thus weaken moral judgment.

How we hold Hitler in memory shapes our sense of historical justice. So, too, does the way we remember Hitler's victims. What we must remember, above all, is what Elie Wiesel singles out:

> It must therefore be said over and over again: Confronted by inhuman executioners, victims suffered and died without betraying their humanity. For every father who, at breaking point, stole from his son, there were 100 who sacrificed themselves for their children. . . . On this human level, the enemy lost. He did not succeed in reducing all his prisoners to the animal state. In the camps and ghettos, there were men who prayed, women who

taught, doctors who healed, poets who sang and made others sing; there were warriors who fought, simple men and woman who fasted on Yom Kippur, and refusing despair, drew on their faith or memory. And yes, there were human beings who rejected cruelty and brutality as instruments of survival: Surely that is a miracle.

And a miracle never to forget.

# CHAPTER  XI

# ART SHAPES REMEMBRANCE

*In memory everything seems to happen to music.*
    —TENNESSEE WILLIAMS

*Now I am wiser: for I know there is not any memory with less satisfaction in it than the memory of some temptation we resisted.*    —JAMES BRANCH CABELL

*Women and elephants never forget.*
    —DOROTHY PARKER

*The things we remember best are those better forgotten.*    —BALTASAR GRACIAN

The part that art plays in establishing memory is fundamental. Most people know "the facts" only about themselves. They learn the facts about everything else secondhand; that is, through the words and images created by others. "With few exceptions," says the critic Alvin Rosenfeld, "we 'see' what we are given to see, 'know' what we are given to know, and thus come to retain in memory what impressed itself on us as vision and knowledge."

Yet not even what we know about ourselves is entirely trustworthy. For memory is treacherous. The other side of it is forgetting, forgetting what we cannot look in the face. When German, Jewish, and Polish survivors try to remember exactly the same event they witnessed in World War II, they simply cannot remember it the same. For each brings to the recall of the event a different experience of it, a different response to it, different pressures that store it intact in the mind, or distort it, or wipe it out.

Art shapes remembrance as well as forgetting. The memory of a creative writer is as subject to errors as anyone else's. Novelists refashion the past, not out of a faithfulness to history, but by following the course of personal feeling—dream, wish, hope. They make out of the "facts" the fiction they desire.

Autobiographers, too. They may think they are writing on oath to themselves to tell the truth, the whole truth, and nothing but the truth. But as the student of a man's life often discovers, what the man wrote about himself is how he wanted to appear. Yet that is important, for how he sees himself, the image of the self he constructs in his life story, is just as much a part of his personality. We all put on masks, finding it useful, necessary, and even fun. So writer after writer, all through literary history, sets down a narrative of half-truths in which memory fails again and again to speak with accuracy. But that does not matter. What the writer is doing is using the past in the revision of the present. He or she has reshaped memory to make life meaningful.

For writers, memory is the quarry they dig into for their material. The Russian novelist Dostoevsky said that he couldn't go on living without memories, especially the precious and sacred memories of childhood. He and other writers have noted that childhood came alive for them only toward the end of their life. It is not that you ever forget it, Thomas De Quincey said, but that "the secret inscriptions of memory are waiting to be revealed when the obscuring daylight shall have been withdrawn."

Another Russian writer, Esther Salaman, speaks of "involuntary memories—those that come back unexpectedly, suddenly, and bring back a past moment accompanied by strong emotions, so that a 'then' becomes a 'now.'" Such memories have been made use of by many writers. Perhaps the best-known example is the French novelist Marcel Proust, in his masterwork, *Remembrance of Things Past*. His method is illustrated in the celebrated incident of the cake, the "madeleine" dipped in tea. Here it is, considerably compressed:

> One day in winter as I came home, my mother, seeing that I was cold, offered me some tea. . . . I raised to my lips a spoonful of the tea in which I had soaked a morsel of the cake. No sooner had the warm liquid, and the crumbs with it, touched my palate than a shudder ran through my whole body. . . . An exquisite pleasure had invaded my senses. . . . Whence could it have come to me, this all-powerful joy? . . . And suddenly the memory returns. The taste was that of the little crumb of "madeleine" which on Sunday mornings at Combray . . . my Aunt Léonie used to give me, dipping it first in her own cup of tea. . . . Immediately the old grey house upon the street rose up like the scenery of a theatre . . . all the flowers in our gar-

den and in Monsieur Swann's park, and the water-
lilies on the Vivonne and the good folk of the vil-
lage . . . and the whole of Combray . . . sprang into
being . . . from my cup of tea.

These unlooked-for memories have been compared
to the way artists and scientists often reach the solution of a problem. It comes as a swift and totally sur-
prising gift from the unconscious mind. While the
conscious mind is taking great care to find the answer,
suddenly the solution appears as if out of nowhere, and
"almost immediately one recognizes its validity and
claims it as one's own."

The writer Alastair Reid has experienced this sensa-
tion and describes it:

Remembering a particular house often brings back
a predominant mood, a certain weather of the
spirit. Sometimes, opening the door of a till then
forgotten room brought on that involuntary
shiver, that awed suspension. These sudden re-
memberings are gifts to writers, like the taste of
the madeleine—for much of writing is simply
finding ways of re-creating astonishments in
words. . . . An instance of remembering can, without warning, turn into a present moment, a total
possession, a haunting.

In her book describing *One Writer's Beginnings*, Eudora Welty relives her own memories—painful as well
as pleasant—and the part they have played in her art.

She calls the individual human memory "that most wonderful interior vision. . . . My own is the treasure most dearly regarded by me, in my life and in my work as a writer. . . . The memory is a living thing—it too is in transit. But during its moment, all that is remembered joins, and lives—the old and the young, the past and the present, the living and the dead."

But how accurate are the memories writers call upon? When he came to write his autobiography in old age, W. E. B. DuBois warned his readers not to take such life stories as indisputable truth. Autobiographies, he said, "are always incomplete, and often unreliable. Eager as I am to put down the truth, there are difficulties; memory fails especially in small details, so that it becomes finally but a theory of my life, with much forgotten and misconceived, with valuable testimony but often less than absolutely true, despite my intention to be frank and fair. . . ."

It usually happens that imagination manipulates memory to create a pattern of experience. Or at least one can say the two intersect. Memory and imagination, in one view, are only facets of the same human faculty. In writing his story, the autobiographer intermingles historic reality with creative dream. The result is a combination of art and history.

How much of memory does the writer hold back when he tells us his personal history? Dostoevsky wrote:

> Every man has reminiscences which he would not tell to everyone, but only to his friends. He has

other matters in his mind which he would not re-
veal even to his friends, but only to himself, and
that is secret. But there are other things which a
man is afraid to tell even to himself, and every decent man has a number of such things stored away
in his mind. The more decent he is, the greater the
number of such things in his mind. . . . A true autobiography is almost an impossibility. . . . Man is
bound to lie about himself.

Another aspect of autobiography to consider is our
own experience in telling people different versions of
something that happened to us long before. Theodore
Rosengarten, who edited *All God's Dangers: The Life
of Nate Shaw*, the taped recollections of a black tenant
farmer from Alabama, heard Shaw "tell a particular
story five or six times to different people. He would
vary a mood, add or omit a detail, shift himself from
foreground to background, to produce the effect he
wanted. He had one version for his family, one for the
neighbors, one for traveling salesmen, and one for
me—and they were all the same story, each told with
the personality of the listener in mind."

Which is the true memory? Or are they all true?

The artist serves a special function when he can
shatter the amnesia of the society or culture he is part
of. Earlier, we saw how totalitarian regimes seek to im-
pose a pattern of conformism upon their people.
Through the system of education, through advertising,
the press, radio, television, movies, books, memory is
controlled. The aim is to prevent any recall of experi-

ence that departs from the dogmas of the dictator.

Writers, especially in repressive societies, bear the burden of trying to bring the truth to their generation. Where there is no freedom of thought or expression, how can there be social justice? Are not debate and diversity essential to truth and progress? Won't the all-powerful rulers—whether of the right or of the left—inevitably manage the society for their own selfish ends? The stories told by writers in such worlds raise these questions in their readers' minds and force them to come to grips with their meaning.

"It is not by chance that so many of the prisoners of conscience for whom Amnesty International works are writers, journalists, or artists," Thomas Hammarberg, Amnesty's secretary general, told an international conference on human rights. "One single poem, one article or book could open eyes closed by millions of propaganda dollars."

The Amnesty group campaigns for the freedom of writers and journalists imprisoned for the nonviolent exercise of their right to free expression. Repressive governments rely on their citizens' ignorance of their human rights or indifference to abuses. When governments don't want information or opinion to be made public through the media, they try to silence writers. In South Korea, for instance, the writer Kim Hyong-Jang was sentenced to life in prison for writing about an army and police action in which several hundred Korean civilians died. In Guatemala, the poet Alaide Foppa de Solorzano was kidnapped by the security forces more than five years ago and is still among the "disappeared."

An interesting sidelight on this story is how imprisoned writers have used memory to help themselves survive. Hiber Conteris, a distinguished Latin American writer, was put in jail in his native Uruguay for eight years, ending in 1985. During a period of severe torture, intended to break him psychologically so that he would sign a confession and not tell the court that he was coerced into it, he found a defense against the ordeal.

As a professor of literature, Conteris had often taught Homer's *Iliad*. One part of the epic poem deals with a Trojan soldier named Dolon who spies on the Greek camp and is captured. They make him confess, then kill him, and use the information obtained to cause great damage to the Trojans.

In his dungeon, Conteris found himself in a similar situation:

> The story of Dolon once again came to my mind, and I began to retell it in my own way, in verse, constructing each day between 12 and 15 strophes in my memory, knowing that I had to do it in verse because that was the only way memory could recall what it was doing. This was an interesting experience, because I had always taught that the hexameter, the Greek verse, was in its origins a mnemonic tool, a way to help the memory when a script was not available, so that poets and

actors, or performers, could recite Homer's lengthy story. In that same way I also found that the poem was the way to help my memory.

By identifying himself with Dolon's story, Conteris was able to forget the soldier who came twice a day to take him to the bathroom and beat him. His literary re-creation of Homer restored his mental balance and helped him through the brutality inflicted upon him.

Another writer—Charlotte Delbo, a French novelist, dramatist, and poet—fell back upon her memory of literature to help herself and other women survive the ordeal of Auschwitz during the Holocaust. She had always liked to memorize the texts of plays, and working in the French theater for some time, she found it came naturally as she watched plays being rehearsed. Later, in the concentration camp, she found herself with cellmates who had never had a chance to see a play. At night, when they had gone to their cells after a long day of inhuman labor, recalls a close friend, Delbo "would lighten their burden by evoking a magic place: a red and gold theater space, a stage from which proud words were spoken to a receptive audience. Charlotte's friends vowed that if they were to survive they would see all the plays she re-created for them. . . ."

As one of her friends, Rosette C. Lamont, put it, "We realize that great art helped people survive because survival in dire circumstances can be a matter of spirit. Only memory makes it possible for prisoners to envision a future."

Various methods are used to silence writers, and artists, too. In the Soviet Union, the government has charged many writers with "anti-Soviet agitation and propaganda" because they tried to exercise their right to free expression. What the Russian leadership especially wants the country to forget is the Stalinist past. This was the years from the 1920s to the early 1950s when the dictator Stalin made slave labor a significant part of the Communist regime. He used millions of political prisoners on a great variety of projects, penning them up in concentration camps. Students of Soviet affairs estimate that from several million to 25 million were victims of the slave labor system.

Death camps have not returned, summary executions are no longer commonplace, and mass repressions are avoided in the Soviet Union now. But men and women are still being committed to jail, to labor camps, to internal exile, to psychiatric prisons, for insisting on their rights as defined in Soviet law, and for defending human rights and their own dignity. A system so monolithic leaves no room for human freedom. The relentless demand for conformity cramps human talents.

Writers understand the power of memory and also how vulnerable it is to pressure. When a society's past comes to be seen as politically mad or personally embarrassing, the temptation by the rulers to blot it out is great.

The official histories of the U.S.S.R. contain glaring omissions and distortions. A hero of one time can become a blank page in the next time. The mistakes or weaknesses of any figure in power can be glossed over or ignored altogether while his virtues are praised beyond belief. It makes the work of the artist all the more important as an avenue by which to explore the truth about the past, and preserve it.

It took great courage for the Soviet poet Yevgeny Yevtushenko to speak out against distortion of history, self-flattery, and silence in the world of Russian literature. At a congress of Russian writers in 1985, he demanded of them the candor and openness that the new Soviet leader, Mikhail S. Gorbachev, had called for in other fields of endeavor. The poet drew great applause when he quoted from Tolstoy, who said: "The epigraph that I would write for history would say: I conceal nothing. It is not enough not to lie. One should strive not to lie in a negative sense by remaining silent." Yevtushenko then pointed out:

> When you read the periodically retouched pages of our modern history, you bitterly see that the pages are interspersed with white spots of silence and concealment, dark spots of obsequious truth-stretching and smudges of distortion. . . . In many textbooks important names and events are arbitrarily excluded. They not only fail to list the reasons for the disappearance of leading people in the party, but sometimes even the date of their death, as if they were peacefully living on pension. . . . Only fearlessness in the face of the past can help to produce a fearless solution to the problems of the present. . . .

Yet the poet's speech on honesty, when reported in a Soviet weekly, was heavily censored. Several major sections were left out, along with all but one comment that appealed for an end to censorship. Other writers at the same meeting echoed the poet's call for openness. Plainly, they hoped Gorbachev would loosen controls on literature and the arts and allow freer expression.

On the other hand, the Soviet government uses every means possible to preserve and keep alive its people's memories of World War II. It has published more than fifteen thousand books on the subject of the war and has erected monuments and memorials in every town. Professor Stephen F. Cohen of Princeton University, a specialist on Soviet affairs, believes that the war, more than any other event, including the Russian Revolution, shaped the Soviet Union as it exists today. For most Americans, that war is a remote and half-forgotten historical event. For Soviet citizens, it was an experience of colossal tragedy and triumph. Fifty Soviet citizens died for every one American. Almost every Soviet family lost one member or more.

The huge Soviet losses in the war, never forgotten, made both government and people unite in the determination that their country would never again be caught unprepared by a surprise attack. It explains their obsession with national security and the high priority given to military expenditures. If Americans understood that collective memory, it might help strengthen the political will to find a way for both great powers to live together in peace.

# GLOSSARY

Relatively few technical terms are used in the text. When they are, they are defined. This short list may be helpful to some readers.

*Amnesia.* Loss of memory due to brain injury, shock, fever, repression. Also, a gap in one's memory.

*Biochemistry.* The chemistry of plant and animal life.

*Cerebral.* Pertaining to the brain, or to the nature of the brain.

*Cognition.* A mental operation by which we become aware of objects of thought or perception, or of a memory.

*Consolidation theory.* The theory which assumes that material is pulled together in the brain after learning. This is said to occur during rest.

*Cortex.* As commonly used, the term refers to the convoluted mass of brain cells comprising the highest brain center. This large outer layer of the brain is in major part responsible for characteristically human behavior.

*Eidetic imagery.* Called "photographic memory" by the layman, it is the abiility to retain an image for a long period of time.

*Glial cells.* Small chemical units in the brain, used as a "screen" and thought to feed or nourish the brain cells.

*Hemisphere.* The cortex is divided into two parts, each of which is called a hemisphere. The right hemisphere is said to be responsible for control of the left side of the body, and the left hemisphere is responsible for control of the right portion of the body.

*Hippocampus.* One of the three major divisions of the human brain, called the forebrain, contains what is called the limbic system. The hippocampus is a structure in the limbic system connected with memory.

*Kinesthetic.* The type of sensory experience derived from the muscle sense, from bodily movements and tensions.

*Korsakoff's syndrome.* A stable, chronic condition of severe memory dysfunction.

*Long-term memory.* Memory retained for a substantial period of time—more than a day, for example.

*Microelectrode.* Very thin, electrically activated wire, used in brain experiments.

*Mnemonic device.* Unusual trick or combination that helps one to remember.

*Mnemonics.* The art of improving the efficiency of the memory; from the Greek *mneme*, the goddess of memory.

*Nerve.* A group of neurons or individual nerve cells that together transmit information.

*Neurochemistry.* The chemistry of the nervous system.

*Neuron.* The individual nerve cell with all its attachments. It is the basic unit of the nervous system, and the fundamental building block of the brain.

*Principle learning.* An effective device for remembering that brings items together under a single unifying system.

*Psychology.* The science that treats of the mind in any of its aspects.

*Short-term memory.* Memory retained for a brief period of time—say, less than a day. If memories are lost at this stage, they do not make it to the long-term storage areas of the brain.

*Synapse.* The junction of two neurons; a locale where a nerve impulse is transmitted from one neuron to another.

*Temporal lobe.* That part of the cerebral cortex beneath the temples of the skull.

# BIBLIOGRAPHY

Andreason, Nancy C. *The Broken Brain: The Biological Revolution in Psychiatry.* New York: Harper & Row, 1984.

Bailey, Ronald H. *Role of the Brain.* New York: Time-Life Books, 1975.

Benjamin, Walter. *Illuminations.* New York: Harcourt Brace Jovanovich, 1968.

Boorstin, Daniel J. *The Discoverers.* New York: Random House, 1983.

Bringuier, Jane Claude. *Conversations with Jean Piaget.* Chicago: University of Chicago Press, 1980.

Buñuel, Luis. *My Last Sigh.* New York: Knopf, 1983.

Buzan, Tony. *Make the Most of Your Mind.* New York: Linden, 1984.

Crick, Francis. "Thinking About the Brain," *Scientific American,* 1984.

Diagram Group. *The Brain: A User's Manual.* New York: Berkley, 1983.

Frazier, Katharine. "Some Hints About Memorizing," *Eolus* (Jan. 1925).

Gardner, Howard. *The Shattered Mind.* New York: Knopf, 1975.

Gerard, Ralph. "What Is Memory?," *Scientific American* (Sept. 1953), 118–26.

Girard, Paul. "Some Prolific Musical Memories," *American Music* (Jan. 1936).

Hall, Edward T. *Beyond Culture.* Garden City, N.Y.: Doubleday/Anchor Press, 1976.

Harris, J. E., and P. E. Morris, eds. *Everyday Memory, Actions and Absent-Mindedness.* New York: Academic Press, 1984.

Hubel, David H. "The Brain." *Scientific American*, 1984.

Hunt, Morton. *The Universe Within.* New York: Simon & Schuster, 1982.

Kemeny, John G. *Man and the Computer.* New York: Scribner's, 1972.

Klatzky, Roberta L. *Memory and Awareness.* San Francisco: W. H. Freeman, 1984.

Lanning, Russell E. "Intelligent Memorizing," *Music Teachers Review* (Nov.–Dec. 1941).

Loftus, Elizabeth F. *Eyewitness Testimony.* Cambridge: Harvard University Press, 1979.

Neisser, Ulric, ed. *Memory Observed: Remembering in Natural Contexts.* San Francisco: W. H. Freeman, 1982.

Nilsson, Lars G., ed. *Perspectives on Memory Research.* Hillsdale, N.J.: Laurence Erlbaum, 1979.

Norman, Donald A. *Learning and Memory.* San Francisco: W. H. Freeman, 1982.

Ornstein, Robert, and Richard F. Thompson. *The Amazing Brain.* Boston: Houghton Mifflin, 1984.

Park, Clara Claiborne. "The Mother of the Muses: In Praise of Memory," *American Scholar* (Winter 1980–81).

Restak, Richard. *The Brain.* New York: Bantam, 1984.

Rosenfeld, Alvin. *Imagining Hitler.* Bloomington: Indiana University Press, 1985.

Rosenfield, Israel. "The New Brain," *New York Review* (Mar. 14, 1985), 34–38.

Russell, Peter. *The Brain Book.* New York: Dutton, 1975.

Russell, W. Ritchie. *Exploring the Brain.* Oxford: Oxford University Press, 1975.

Sacks, Oliver. "The Twins," *New York Review* (Feb. 28, 1985), 16–20.

Sagan, Carl. *The Dragons of Eden.* New York: Random House, 1977.

Smith, Anthony. *The Mind.* New York: Viking, 1984.

Smith, Brian. *Memory.* London: Allen & Unwin, 1966.

Spence, Donald B. *Narrative Truth and Historical Truth.* New York: Norton, 1982.

Spence, Jonathan D. *The Memory Palace of Matteo Ricci.* New York: Viking, 1984.

Stone, Albert E. *Autobiographical Occasions and Original Acts.* Philadelphia: University of Pennsylvania Press, 1982.

Tapper, Thomas. "How to Capitalize Music Memory." *Etude* (April 1940).

Welty, Eudora. *One Writer's Beginnings.* Cambridge: Harvard University Press, 1983.

Yates, Frances A. *The Art of Memory.* London: Penguin, 1969.

# INDEX

## About the Book

You probably think you have a poor memory. You forget your mother's birthday, you can't recall the year the Civil War started. But you can recognize the faces of everyone in your class when you meet them on the street. You know the words and music of dozens of rock songs. . . . Even the most ordinary mind has a fantastic capacity for memory.

Exploring how we remember and why we forget opens up a world of paradoxes. How can the brain, "the three-pound marvel," store more information than the world's largest computer, yet fail to solve a simple problem? Then, just when you forget the problem, you remember the answer! How can *not* studying actually help you remember your assignment? Why does a certain smell release a flood of long-lost memories, clearer than the events of yesterday?

Milton Meltzer, the "renowned author of nonfiction" (*Publishers Weekly*), explores the complexities of memory, from the interior landscape of an individual's memory to the wider vistas of cultural and historical memory. He tells of the man with no memory, the man who could not forget, and other fascinating case histories and anecdotes. Far-reaching and perceptive, *The Landscape of Memory* offers a thought-provoking look at the greatest asset of the human mind.

## About the Author

Milton Meltzer says, "I wrote this book out of several impulses. One was observing the gradual loss of memory that signaled the sad onset of Alzheimer's disease in people close to me. As an author of books on history and biography, I make constant forays into memory, both individual and collective. I wanted to share with readers some of these experiences.

"I started work on this book, knowing little of what science has learned about memory. What I found out added greatly to my understanding, but made me realize how much mystery there still is in the almost magical way memory performs."

Milton Meltzer's more than sixty books for children and adults include four biographies in the *Women of Our Time*™ series. He is now working on a book about his growing-up years in Worcester, Massachusetts. He and his wife, parents of two grown daughters, live in New York City.